FIRST DANGLE
AND OTHER STORIES

FIRST DANGLE
AND OTHER STORIES

kevin hearne

Horned Lark Press

First Dangle and Other Stories
Cover Art Copyright © 2017 by Galen Dara
First Dangle, "The Naughtiest Cherub, "The Waters," and "Friendly Emily"

© 2019 by Kevin Hearne

A Horned Lark Press Book
Published by Horned Lark Press
1087-2482 Yonge Street
Toronto, ON M4P 2H5

www.hornedlarkpress.com

Reprinted Edition.
ISBN: 978-1-998390-00-7

Interior Design and Formatting:
www.emtippettsbookdesigns.com

Printed in a Secret Volcano Lair by Antifascist Capybaras

By Kevin Hearne

The Seven Kennings

A Plague of Giants

A Blight of Blackwings

A Curse of Krakens

The Iron Druid Chronicles

Hounded	*Hunted*
Hexed	*Shattered*
Hammered	*Staked*
Tricked	*Besieged*
Trapped	*Scourged*

The Iron Druid Chronicles Novellas

Two Ravens and One Crow	*A Prelude to War*
Grimoire of the Lamb	*First Dangle and Other Stories*

Oberon's Meaty Mysteries

The Purloined Poodle

The Squirrel on the Train

The Buzz Kill

The Chartreuse Chanteuse

INK & SIGIL

Ink & Sigil

Paper & Blood

Candle & Crow

OTHER NOVELLAS

A Question of Navigation

The Hermit Next Door

BY DELILAH S. DAWSON AND KEVIN HEARNE

TALES OF PELL

Kill the Farm Boy

No Country for Old Gnomes

The Princess Beard

www.kevinhearne.com

THE NAUGHTIEST CHERUB

This story, narrated by Loki, takes place directly before the events of Scourged, *book 9 of the Iron Druid Chronicles. Originally printed in the* Urban Enemies *anthology.*

The road to hell is not, as they say, paved with good intentions. Mostly it's crumbling stone, some rank weeds, and the occasional pile of dog shit. At least the one I am following is; there are many roads to perdition, but this one is in Kansas for some reason. And I will note for the record that there is a significant difference between going to Hel and going to hell.

My daughter's realm, for all that it is cold and dim and cheerless with a constant cover of damp clouds, is at least somewhat consistent in its conception and manifestation.

The hell of monotheists, by contrast, is a hot, shifting, poisonous plane with air so foul that it feels as bad on my skin as it smells—that is, polluted with all manner of evils. As soon as I step through a portal created by an obliging demon, my armpits begin to sweat goat cheese and my balls feel like they're marinating in pepper sauce. I am blasted by hot dry winds and chapped by sulfurous fumes one moment, and in the next buffeted by a moist effluvium shat from some manky demon's ass upwind.

Or perhaps the source of the miasma is not that far away at all, but rather my hellspawn escort, guiding me to a meeting with Lucifer.

"What am I looking at, here?" I ask it—and I use "it" because I am not sure that it has a gender or even a functioning set of reproductive organs. It's a four-legged doglike thing except that its legs are designed like those of an insect, originating underneath the beast and splayed out to the side, and it is painted like an insect too, all green and teal. "Is this the hell of Milton, Dante, or Hieronymous Bosch, perhaps? Scenes out of a Doré etching?"

"You've done your research. It is all those and more," it replies, in a voice that sounds like he's chewing on rock salt yet somehow finds it sour. "There are circles of hell. There are realms of darkness. There is a lake of fire. There are dukes of hell, and imps and hellhounds and most anything collectively imagined by humans."

My escort is decidedly from the Bosch lineup of hellions. "And the being I will be visiting shortly? How does he appear?"

"However he wishes. I have seen him take many forms."

"Interesting."

"Do you not take many forms? I have heard you have the power to do so."

"I do. I do indeed. But they are forms that I imagine, rather than forms that have been imagined by others. They are not my natural manifestation, merely a suit of clothes, so to speak, that I wear for a short time."

The landscape—or hellscape—wobbles in front of me as if I had drunk too much mead, then snaps back together with an audible pop, looking sharp and threatening as the tip of Odin's spear.

"What just happened?" I ask the thing.

"Hell constantly readjusts itself according to the fevered imaginations of mortals."

"Does this happen in heaven too?"

"I'm sure I wouldn't know. Maybe the clouds move around or something. I suspect it is not so richly imagined as hell."

When I am finally brought before Lucifer as arranged, he does not appear in any form close to popular conception. No horns on his head with a pointy mustache and soul patch. No forked tail or trident or any weapon at all. No goat hooves or ram's head, damn it—I was rather hoping to see that one. No suave good looks, and certainly no leathery bat wings. There are wings, however, four massive ones, which take turns flapping and hiding his spherical body from view, keeping most of his bulk shielded from sight as he slowly rotates in place only five feet above ground. What's he hiding under there? Tiny dinosaur arms? An embarrassing angelic erection? A series of mouths and other orifices? Mostly all I see are eyes. Many eyes, black and winking at me with jeweled eyelids, always three or more trained on me as he spins and flaps and waits.

The wings are not merely attractive: they are glorious. Shiny, shimmering, and rippling with a spectrum of colors, prismatic coyness that defies simple description. It is, no doubt, why humans took to describing him with more beastlike qualities. Cherubs are beautiful and difficult to imagine as an agent of evil. And Lucifer was—and remains—the most powerful and beautiful of the cherubim.

Such sublime magnificence is far more intimidating than any bestial appearance he could have taken, and as soon as I think it I know that is why he chose to appear that way.

"Lucifer, I bring Loki of the Æsir, who seeks audience," the demon says. I am surprised and pleased that he keeps the introductions so short. We do not need a long list of titles and ego fluffing. We know who we are.

~*What do you wish to ask me*? Lucifer says. The words do not come from him so much as the air around my ears, a chorus of deep musical voices rather than a single one.

"Your aid, as you no doubt have surmised. The Norns are dead, killed by a lucky Druid, and I am no longer doomed to suffer defeat in Ragnarok. Fate no longer applies to me and I, along with many others, may choose my own."

~So?

"So we who desire to play a different role than what we've been assigned may seize this opportunity to sweep aside the current world order and forge a better one. I have already secured the assurances of many others who will act when Ragnarok begins, and your help will ensure our collective victory."

~Oh, yes. I know of your machinations. These eyes see much. But I am not one to indulge in collective victories. I am not what humans would call a 'team player.' I am the adversary.

The blanket statement disturbs me. "Surely not *my* adversary?"

~Not yet.

That's not reassuring. "Does that mean you may become my adversary later?"

~It remains to be seen. As you said, a significant aspect of fate has been unchained. What will happen cannot be told.

"If I begin Ragnarok, then, what should I expect from you?"

~You may not expect my aid, Loki Firestarter. It may come should it amuse me at the time, but do not count on it.

"May I at least hope you will not interfere?"

~You may not. I may also find interference amusing. At this point I am primarily interested in amusement. The world is going to hell largely without my involvement, and that has been most entertaining to watch. The chaos increased significantly after the deaths of David Bowie and Prince in 2016.

"Who?"

~Bah! Mediocre. I am revising what I said earlier: You may not expect my aid at all. I have no interest in your dreams of power. Whether you win or lose, I shall remain as I am: Puissant. Sexy. The naughtiest cherub.

My mouth gapes at his words and something flies in, diving down my throat. It's hot and squirming and tickles and I begin to hack desperately to get it out. Something eventually gets ejected—a many-legged winged creature with a tiny human head, teal and green and still alive. It hacks and coughs too, suffers through some high-pitched wheezing, and then it shakes itself free of phlegm and saliva and giggles. At the same time, Lucifer's wings shudder and he wobbles slightly in the air.

~Hurr hurr. Hah, he laughs. At my expense. Because he had probably set the whole thing up. Say something shocking to make my jaw drop and a minor demon dives in to make me choke. Very well.

"Apologies for taking up so much of your time, Lucifer. I will not waste any more of it."

~Nonsense. I was amused. But do be careful upon your exit. Some of hell's creatures are jealous and have been known to attack those who have spoken to me personally.

I nod, not trusting myself to say anything diplomatic, and turn to exit the way I entered.

"Not that way," the dog insect says. "That road's closed now. You never leave the same way you came in. Follow me."

My muscles tense but I follow, seeing little other choice. Perhaps it is an ambush he leads me to. Perhaps I will have a chance to pay someone back for the humiliation I just suffered. Once out of sight of Lucifer, I change myself to the shape of a true fire giant and set my skin aflame. I pull out two weapons I had hidden before: a tremendous bastard sword which I also set alight, and an unusual ice knife crafted by the yeti that I stole from the young Druid, Granuaile MacTiernan. Even in the blistering furnace of hell it remains frozen and unmelting.

Satisfied that I look nothing like my usual self and quite a bit more intimidating, I keep scanning my surroundings for possible threats and follow the Bosch nightmare.

It's fine, honestly, that Lucifer will not be joining us. If he stays out of Ragnarok, chances are his opposite will stay out of it too. It's simply not the Christian pantheon's fight. But I think he's wrong that he'll be the same afterward. There will be significantly fewer believers of his particular faith afterward and his power will necessarily wane.

Something moves in my peripheral vision and I look up and to my right. There's a creature much larger than the green and teal thing descending from above. He has bat wings and a humanoid body with a giant dangly snake between his legs and eyes that glow pale yellow. When he sees that I've spotted him, hellfire blooms from his outstretched hand. I point my sword at him and send a gout to block his incoming one. Neither of us will be burned but there is a certain kinetic force behind such attacks, and I'd rather he be off balance than me when it comes to melee. He has no weapons except for some wicked claws and probably twice the brute strength I possess. Those wings will no doubt cause some trouble too. Another muscle-bound bully like Thor.

I keep the sword raised and pointed at him just in case he's stupid enough to fly onto it, but he turns off the fire, folds those wings in, and veers to my left. More difficult for me to guard against that way with the sword in my right hand. I have seen this before in fighting against some of the Fae: there is a claw on the tip of his wing, and as he sails past on the left, he will open those wings and try to cut me with it. He's going to be about at neck level, aiming for my throat, so I take a knee and thrust up with that ice knife as the wing shoots out and over my head. It pierces the leathery membrane and I hold it there as his own momentum forces it to tear through his wing.

I expect a cry of rage and a ferocious counterattack on foot afterward, but instead I get a startled squawk and the damned thing crashes to the sandblasted ground, dead.

The demon dog is agog, and he's not the only one.

"How did you do that?" it asks.

"I don't know. I just sliced his wing."

"With what? He's died the final death. Look, already he shrivels."

It's true: The creature had been a tomato-red steroidal horror straight out of the nightmares of medieval humans, but now it is dissolving and bubbling into a puddle of black tar. I look down at the ice knife and see that it is different: Colder, giving off steam while still remaining frozen solid, and the thin crimson glow along the top of the blade extends all the way to the point and pulses with energy.

"I think this knife may have drunk its soul. Do demons have souls?"

"Some do. He certainly did. Where did you get that knife?"

"Never mind that," I snap at it. "Just get me out of here before something else comes along."

"Of course."

I had not paid close enough attention to this weapon when I stole it. How had the yeti learned such magic? And why, if they possessed such secrets, had they shared them with Granuaile MacTiernan, the gullible Druid? Though I must admit I underestimated her. She managed to put an axe in my back and stole the white horse of Świętowit from me, giving him to some witches in Poland with very strong wards around their property. My shoulder still aches as a reminder of how arrogant I'd been. These Druids are dangerous if given a chance to act and deserve more respect than I'd given them to this point. Perhaps the yeti know better than I. Perhaps I should persuade the yeti to make more of these knives before Ragnarok begins. But I have found the lost arrows of Vayu, which never miss their target. I have this soul-drinking blade. And I have many allies and surprises besides. The world is bigger than when the Norns first prophesied Ragnarok. Happily, my plans have grown to meet this new world, and I think we are ready. Or at least as ready as we will ever be. Assessing where Lucifer stands was the last errand to run.

"How much farther do we have to go?" I ask my guide.

"Some distance, unfortunately. At least an hour of subjective time."

It had not been an hour's walk to reach Lucifer. "You're trying to make sure I never leave, aren't you?"

"No! I am positive Lucifer wishes you to remain alive. He is interested in your project, even if he doesn't wish to participate."

"My *project?* You are calling Ragnarok a mere *project?*"

"Please forgive my poor choice of words. I have no proper appreciation for the scale of things and do not even know what

Ragnarok is. In any case, regarding the greater demon you just slew, you did precisely as you should have. Let us continue and remain vigilant."

"Where will this put me on Earth?"

"This particular maw of hell we are using will empty into what the humans call New Jersey."

"Hmm. I have heard of it. By all reports, more hellish than other places on the human plane. But a significant distance from Kansas if I am not mistaken." I had been studying maps of the modern world in recent days. "More than a mere hour's walk."

"The space here is fluid, as you have no doubt seen."

Yes, I'd seen that. Even as the demon dog speaks, the horizon melts and wobbles in my vision, resolves into a slightly different hellscape with red peaks shifted and plumes of ash and lava billowing elsewhere than they did mere seconds ago, yet the path we follow remains. I maintain my giant form but add spider eyes to my head, which always gives me a headache from interpreting so much visual information, but as it will provide me with views of the sky and my trail, I cannot afford to remain limited by human vision.

Lucifer let me go far too easily and this demon escort is far too placating: I am being set up for slaughter. Probably being led into a trap. It's not paranoia because someone really did try to kill me. And there will be more attempts, I have no doubt. Lucifer has absolved himself of responsibility by claiming that they are rogues, but it is beyond belief that visiting gods to his realm can be attacked without his approval. If he were truly concerned for my welfare, he would escort me out himself.

Off to my right, in a hollow between low mesas baked to a blood-orange crisp, a shadow flickers, then moves. It is in fact many shadows, cast by a boiling army of imps lurching in my direction. These cannot *all* be silly homicidal rogues out to cause some mischief in my general area. Someone ordered them to froth and foam in my direction. And I will need more than two arms to defeat them. More than two weapons, in fact. And thank the giants of Muspellheim for teaching me to always have them on hand. Or rather, have them stowed safely.

A fantastic benefit of being able to change one's shape is the ability to store weapons in orifices that would be lethal to others. My flesh is both mutable and elastic, and thus my colon contains all kinds of shit. Actual shit, of course, but also other things that I can pull out of there when needed. And I needed everything if I was going to meet a small army of hellions by myself. I also needed a shape that could handle it.

While spending time with Jörmungandr, the world serpent, I learned of many creatures of the sea one can combine to form powerful chimeras. I shifted only above the waist to a mantis shrimp—not really a mantis or a shrimp at all, but it looks similar to both—except that I grew tentacles out to the sides to brandish all the weapons I pulled out of my nether regions. Including the two I already had, I now set myself up with four blades total and these fascinating chitinous limbs that work on a locking latch principle that delivers tremendous kinetic force when released. I can punch anything, basically, that gets close to my face, shattering it without harming myself in the process. My hope is that nothing will get that close.

The imps are a motley collection of shapes, bipedal but otherwise sporting a varied number of limbs, heads, and teeth. Some of them carry hatchets, some have swords, and a couple are very pleased to have found scythes, judging by the number of rotting teeth they show me. Their skin is painted in any of four different pigments but I don't know if the red, green, blue, and black signify any sort of impish hierarchy. They do not approach in any ranks, but rather in a rabid horde—a small horde of thirty or forty, I'm guessing, allied against one, since I notice my escort is scuttling away to keep out of it.

I get to feel confident and superior for all of five seconds, as my lengthened arms take out the vanguard and then the next few as well. But the imps keep barreling forward, counting on their numbers to overwhelm me, and it's a fine reckoning. I stab as fast as I can, black ichor spilling from them and unholy screeches tearing the air, but it's only a second more and their weapons are biting into my chitin, hollow thunks that sting but fail to penetrate to my vitals. The weapons get lodged there and while the imps try to pull them free I stab them and they fall away. I backpedal fast as I can, attempting to give my arms more room to dispatch them at a distance, but it's not as effective as I hoped. They're already too close and they leap at me. One vaults over the others with a hatchet aimed at the space between my eyes, and I let the chitin shrimp hammers fly at him. He crunches without time to squawk, his skull and ribs shattered as he flies back into the press of his fellows, but I don't get to enjoy it for more than a fraction of a second as one of my tentacles is lopped off by a scythe and a bolt of pain lances through my body. The tentacle's nerves fire on the ground and it writhes with one of the shit-covered swords in its grip, and while there are no bones inside it's a pound or two of flesh I'm going to miss.

The ice knife is no more effective than a regular knife against these creatures. They have no souls, apparently, so I must stab into something necessary, not merely prick them with the tip. I discover this when one of them recovers from a stab to the gut to make a screaming charge and hack at my thigh with a hatchet. I fall onto the blistered, scalloped rocks and the imps follow me there, determined to end me. I fear they might not be successful.

I lash out again with the shrimp fists and that launches three crushed bodies into the air, but there are more doing their best to penetrate my chitin and more piling on top of that. I won't be getting up on that leg with an ax buried in it. Time to change tactics by changing shapes.

Choosing yet another shape I learned from Jörmungandr, I become a small sphere of protected organs surrounded on all sides by long spines, something called a sea urchin—except far larger than the real ones you'd find in the ocean. I won't be able to maintain it for long, but I don't need to: It impales every single imp covering me, and when I shift again, the spines slide out of them and their bodies provide me some cover from the remaining imps, who are not sure what happened to their target. I launch myself out of the pile of dead reconstituted as a spider monkey, one of the most acrobatic creatures I've ever seen. I retrieve the ice knife and a sword with my long arms, balancing on them and my one good leg, and proceed to dance among the ten or so remaining imps, chest heaving with oxygen debt and enervated by the shifts and blood loss, hyperaware that I have no natural armor in this form. Metal slices through flesh with slithering noises and howls rise into the fuckfurnace of hell as I spin, slash, and stab through opponents too surprised by my shift to understand what's happening. And when the last one collapses, I fall onto my ass, exhausted and unable to get a breath of clean air, it being actual hell outside. The imps' bodies bubble and hiss as they melt into sludge, and I see my bug-dog guide skitter forward to congratulate me.

"Masterful, sir, simply masterful! May I help in any way?"

I shift back into my accustomed human form, which allows speech instead of unintelligible screeches. "You can insert your head into the anus of a rhinoceros and take a deep breath."

The hellspawn looks around at the blasted land, helpless. "Should one appear, I will do my best, sir."

"Just get me to the nearest exit."

"Certainly. Please follow me."

I collect all my weapons from the ruin of the imp horde and limp after him, my head constantly craning about me, looking for new threats. None appear, and it's almost more nerve-wracking than if something concrete materialized to attack.

Uncountable moments of heat and pain later, the hellspawn stops and raises an insect leg at the air in front of it.

"Here we are, sir. Just a moment." He mutters something unintelligible, his leg spasms in a pattern that must have some arcane significance, and the air puckers and warps in front of him before a rectangle shimmers and resolves into a window to the plane of Midgard.

Just as the portal pops into solid reality and I feel a cool gust of air from New Jersey that is no doubt putrid by human standards but qualifies as a benediction in hell, Lucifer appears to my left, unfolding himself out of the air in a flutter of cherubic feathers. I ready the ice knife in case he attacks.

"What now?" I bark at him.

~I merely wished to congratulate you on making it this far. Perhaps you will have more luck in your rebellion than I thought. I will not aid you, but as you have earned my respect, neither will I hinder you. Seriously, though: you need to get a clue about

David Bowie and Prince. You missed quite a bit being bound for all those years in the bowels of the earth. Before you decide to burn it all down and start over, take some time to appreciate creative geniuses. For you wish to be one, correct?

"A creative genius? No, that is not among my ambitions."

~If I'm not being too forward, Loki, perhaps it should be. My father was a creative genius, much as I despise him. I hear Odin is too. Quite a few of the beings I presume you'll be fighting against are creative geniuses. It would be wise to know your enemy, if nothing else. But also wise to have a plan to build your utopia once the day is won.

"I have a plan. No need to worry about that."

~Ah. Fair enough. Well, then. It's all very exciting, isn't it? This should be good. I'm off to make some popcorn. Metaphorically speaking, of course. Cherubim cannot actually process genemod corn—oh, never mind.

The wings fold around him, he spins like a top in the air until he shrinks and pops out of existence. What a strange adversary.

I'm left alone with the Bosch horror who did nothing to help me—not even provide so much as a warning—against Lucifer's ambushes. I'd like to try out the ice knife on him and see if he has a soul it can drink. The heat of hell has taxed the blade; the red reservoir along the top has noticeably diminished during our trek. It looks thirsty.

"Please step through," the hellion says. "I can only keep the portal open for a few more moments."

Ah, clever to remind me of that. I can't afford to risk being trapped here. I nod as a measure of insincere thanks and step through to New Jersey. The portal closes behind me, and good riddance. If a large portion of humanity can imagine such a creature as Lucifer and a realm as bleak as hell, then Ragnarok will be a merciful fate by comparison.

Time to get on with it.

FIRST DANGLE
An Owen and Slomo Story

Printed for the first time here, this story takes place some months after the events of Scourged, *Book 9 of the Iron Druid Chronicles, and directly before the events of* Ink & Sigil.

CHAPTER 1

Me father used to say, "From bollocks we came," and… that was it. A pun, a confounding of expectations, and his comment on humanity's basic character in four words. He was a frugal man. He'd never say "less is more" when he could simply say "less" and let ye figure out the rest on your own.

I'm starting to think this entire fecking era I'm living in now is trying to repudiate me father's frugality. "More" is the word people live by now. Which is not necessarily a bad thing if you're talking about more dogs or more attention to the damage being done to the earth in pursuit of ever more material comforts, but that's not, unfortunately, what I'm talking about.

What I'm seeing is more waste, more pollution and consumption, and more people worrying about lines they've drawn on a map and who's on which side of those lines than the shared planet they're living on. More blindness to the basic fact that all creatures are part of Gaia and if humans want more of the planet's finite resources then that means less for other creatures, and that's the sort of behavior that leads to the mass extinctions we're suffering now.

What we truly need more of are Druids and I'm working on making that happen, but it's a long process. In the meantime, it's basically me and Granuaile looking after things; she's taken the eastern hemisphere, because she's off training with some guy named Sun Wukong in Taiwan, and I've got the west.

Siodhachan, me old apprentice, can't shift planes anymore, so he's assigned himself the role of taking on long-term projects in a specific area. Right now he's trying to finish up healing Tasmanian devils and then he's going to do something in Australia so he can keep on having flat whites for breakfast.

What it all means is that elementals are coming to me now when they want help. And the planet's so cocked up of late that the cries for help are nearly constant. It's tough to get me teaching in sometimes. But luckily I have the Flagstaff pack pitching in with languages and the like, and all that I am required to be present for is the instruction in Gaia's mysteries and the cultivation of headspaces.

That allows me some brief windows of time in which I can visit a friend of mine in Peru.

Her name is Slomo and she's a winsome lass, cute and kind and covered with bugs and constantly amazed by the wonder and beauty of Gaia. She is a delightful three-toed murder sloth. Together we fight environmental crime.

I left me apprentices playing with their wolfhound puppies—Granuaile had given the grove Orlaith's entire litter—and shifted myself to the rain forest where Slomo lived.

Slomo? I called out mentally as the humidity of the Amazon basin squeegeed itself around my skin. *Are ye awake? It's Owen.*

<Whaa? Oh, hey Oaken!> She calls me that and I rather like it. The elementals picked up on it, in fact, and it pleases me to be called Oaken Druid now instead of Avenging Druid.

Where are ye? Can ye make some noise? Shout a word in Slothian and then tell me what it means.

"Aboblamohno!" her high-pitched voice called out from somewhere to my right. Her vocals were much higher than the mental voice I typically heard.

Uh. Say that again?

"Aboblamohno!" she repeated and that gave me a better bead on her location.

What does that mean?

Slomo's language is a marvel to me. She can talk to trees, apparently, which requires staying in the tree for days at a time. Sloths are one of the few creatures that hang around long enough to have a conversation with them. But in terms of human language she doesn't really know any yet. I figure out what she intends through our mental bond, a combination of thoughts and emotions and images, and put it into words for me own convenience. <It means adventure! Are we going to have one?>

Well, sure. It's a bonny day. It would be a shame to waste it.

<I can't see you yet. Are you almost here?>

I can't see you either. Shout for me one more time?

<Aboblamohno!>

Ah, I think I'm close. Ye should be able to see or hear me soon.

"Excuse me, Eoghan Ó Cinneadie."

I recognized the voice from behind me and winced. "Oh, great blistered badger tits!" I said as I turned around to confirm it was in fact the Herald Extraordinary of Brighid, First among the Fae.

"There are no badger mammary glands of any kind in this forest. I hope you weren't referring to me."

"Coriander the Infinitely Unpunchable," I said. "Why are ye here and why do ye look like that?"

Normally he wore Brighid's livery and looked very proper and extra stuffy, no doubt owing to the powdered curly wig he wore on his head. Now he looked like he had stepped away from his corporate day job and into a sex club where they handed out magic mushrooms like after-dinner mints. He had an androgynous look to him—that being a fancy term that Greta taught me recently. Gender, she said, was viewed as a spectrum now—and I think it was back in me own time, too, it's just that people had gotten better in the last two thousand years at developing new words for what had been true all along. She showed me pictures of David Bowie dressing somewhere in the middle of the spectrum and Cate Blanchett doing the same, just to illustrate the principle. Coriander currently looked a bit something like the latter, dressed in grey tweed slacks and waistcoat over a white long-sleeved shirt with a silver paisley tie and no jacket. His feet were bare and his head sported a blond tousled mess. His cheeks were flush and his big blue eyes wobbled with tears threatening to make a run for it.

"I was on recreational leave just now," he replied, "thus I am not in my accustomed raiment."

"That's how ye dress for recreation?"

"Yes. I find it frolicsome."

"Ye may have a different idea of what frolicking means than most people."

"Of that I have no doubt. I am here to solicit your aid in a matter that is very important to me. My gratitude would be bounteous if you could help."

"What's this? Ye're not here at Brighid's request?"

"No. As I said, I am on leave. This is personal."

"And so ye came to me?"

"I know that seems odd and I freely admit you were not my first choice. But I cannot ask the Tuatha Dé Danann to intervene in this matter and I cannot trust the Fae to be discreet."

<Hey Oaken, are you still out there?>

I am! I got interrupted and will be there soon.

<Okay. I can hang out. That was my whole plan for the day anyway.>

The herald had piqued my interest. "All right, what is the matter?"

"Two humans are dead by what I fear are diabolical means."

"Diabolical, ye say? As in devils from one o' them monotheist hells?"

"I know not which hell—it could be some polytheist demon. Or not. Perhaps even a deity of some kind. Or a creature of some horrible mythology not properly assigned to oblivion. But I am sure this was not done by any human or beast of this plane."

"Huh. And what is your interest in these humans that ye would track me here to ask for help—how did ye find me here, anyway?"

"The Extraordinary bit of my title as Herald Extraordinary means I must be able to find beings who might have some business with the First among the Fae. It is a vital part of my office."

"All right. Who are these humans?"

"Maria and Javier Garces in Granada, Spain."

"Spain? That's the colonial power that messed up this country, isn't it? Destroyed hundreds of species of potatoes in the process?"

"Yes, I believe that is correct."

"Spain is in the eastern hemisphere, right? That's Granuaile's territory. Ye should be talking to her."

"She is…indisposed."

"Indisposed? Are ye tellin' me she's on the toilet so ye came to fetch me to the other side of the planet? Just wait. She'll be flushing before ye know it."

"She is…going to be busy some time."

"Bad seafood, eh?"

"No, that's not it at all. Please just trust me when I say you are my only hope at the moment."

"Ye must be fecking desperate."

The tears that had threated to spill down his cheeks finally did and his voice broke on a sob. "I am. Eoghan. I know we have not had the easiest of relationships but I am hoping you will find a soft place in your heart and decide to aid me."

"I might, lad, I might. Tell me why ye care about the deaths of Maria and Javier Garces."

"Well, as I said," Coriander began, and his eyes shifted away and I knew he was going to dodge the question. *Prevaricate* is the fancy word. "They were slain by diabolical means."

"That's not what has ye cryin' about them. You've seen plenty of death before. So tell me why these deaths have ye gibberin' at me face."

The herald's chin raised, his eyes shining with defiance. "They were my friends."

They were probably more than that. "Both of them?"

"Aye, both!"

"Easy, now. I'm not judging, just tryin' to be clear. Good on ye, lad. Now, I have three questions for ye, until I think of more. First, were Maria and Javier aware that you're Fae?"

Coriander nodded. "They were."

"Were they different from normal humans in any way? Magic users, descendants of gods, anything like that?"

"Maria was an accomplished witch and Javier a slightly less powerful warlock."

"Interesting. And where were they killed? In the city, a remote farm, or what?"

"Outdoors in the Sierra de Huétor Natural Park. A secluded portion of it."

"Ah, perfect. That means I can bring me murder sloth along."

Coriander's jaw dropped. "I beg your pardon?"

"Wait here a couple minutes." I called mentally to my friend. *Hey, Slomo, want to go to Spain with me and have an aboblamohno?*

<Sure, Oaken! Do they have trees in Spain?>

I guarantee it.

CHAPTER 2

oriander left a marker for me so I could follow him to a tethered tree in Spain. Once we got there, Slomo barfed delicately on my shoulder as she always does. Something about shifting planes has that effect on her.

<Sorry,> she said. <I wish that didn't happen.>

Me too, love. But only because I don't want ye to feel bad, ye understand. I don't mind the mess, ye know. It's more important to me that we get to see the world together.

<It's important to me too, Oaken! So I don't mind the upset stomach as long as we get to see new places.>

What do ye think of this place?

<The air is different.>

Not as humid, ye mean?

<Well, yeah, but that's not all. It has a smell. A flavor. It's almost spicy.>

That might be all the blood.

<Oh yeah. That would explain it.>

There was an awful lot of blood. Also vital organs and ropes of intestine snaking on the ground. Chunks and splinters of bone. But absolutely no skin or hair.

"I've seen some feckin' grim butchery in my time, lad, but nothing like this. It's like…"

"They were turned inside out," Coriander finished.

"That's right. That's exactly it."

"So you see why I think no human or beast could have done this."

"I do. Your point is well made. I'm assuming you found them like this?"

"Yes. I was supposed to meet them here and…this is what I found."

"So no clothes, no electronics, nothing of the kind?" I asked, since I saw none of that.

"No."

"Forgive me for asking then: How do ye know that this is Maria and Javier? Ye can't really identify them by this mess."

"I know it in the same way that I know that Siodhachan Ó Suilebháin is playing with his hounds in Tasmania right now and Granuaile is still…indisposed."

"Stay the bloody hell away from shellfish, lad, if ye don't wanna suffer the same fate. That's free advice and it's good, too."

"I assure you that's not what's going on."

"Fine, lad, fine. So ye were supposed to meet Maria and Javier here. Were ye on time or late?"

"On time."

"So they were early. Did ye see anything when ye got here besides them?"

"No."

"No strange noises like a kid yodeling in the distance? Anything at all beside what I'm lookin' at right now?

"No."

"Okay. So either they were targeted by someone who wanted to kill them or it was someone who wanted to strike at you."

"Me?" Clearly the idea had never occurred to him.

"Of course. You're warded tougher than steel-plated rhino horn. Untouchable, unpunchable you, right? So to get at you, someone strikes at those you love."

"But…no one knew. Not even Brighid. I was careful."

"Could no one divine your connection to them?"

"I don't believe so. I think if anyone knew about my relationship…well, they would have had to learn it from them."

"And that's entirely possible, isn't it? Either by guile or divination? Or were they so powerful that they could ward against divination adequately?"

Coriander's eyes glazed over as he considered the question and I took the opportunity to get Slomo situated.

Are ye ready to establish First Dangle in Spain?

<Oh, wow, you bet, Oaken! What kind of tree is this big one here?>

It's a common oak. The tree in question spread gnarled branches over the puddles of gore and its canopy sheltered it from the sun—a minor blessing, I suppose. It meant the smell had only attracted half a swarm of flies so far instead of a full one.

Slomonomobrodolie accepted my boost and wrapped her clawed appendages around a low-hanging branch. She swayed there gently and a smile spread on her face.

<I! Have achieved! First! Danglllllle!> she crowed.

Ye are peerless among slothkind, I said.

<But hey, Oaken, it's really spicy up here. I mean the smell is worse up here than it was on your shoulders. Is that how smell is supposed to work? Because I thought a bad-smelling thing smelled worse the closer you got to it, not the other way around.>

That's a good point. Let me think on that, I said, and tried to figure out what she meant by spicy—she wasn't using that word, mind, it's just the closest term I could think of to attach to her thoughts. She must perceive smells very differently if she didn't think the scene was positively rotten, though.

"I don't think Maria and Javier could protect themselves adequately from someone truly powerful," Coriander said. "I mean, obviously. But I also can't imagine why they would have attracted such attention."

"But *you* would have, eh? You've got some enemies in the hot and sticky places. Been flippin' the bird at demons on Brighid's behalf for lifetimes, haven't ye?"

Coriander's eyes dropped. "Yes," he said, his voice sullen.

"Have ye worn that wig the whole time? Because I tell ye lad, it's infuriating. Demons have even shorter tempers than I do and that wig invites a throttlin' and that's no lie. I like ye without it."

"How does that help, Eoghan? Honestly?"

"Tell me who's been getting themselves in a snit lately. Demons ain't the patient sort to wait and bide their time. If they want to come at ye, they'll do it quickly like a pair o' caffeinated jackrabbits."

"Well, there's the Puritans in hell—"

"The Puritans in hell? Sounds like a band name."

"The ones who weren't predestined members of the Elect. I had to deliver some unpleasant news to Goody Goodneck and she became rather incensed with me."

"She's mad at you instead of whoever feckin' named her Goody Goodneck? Never mind. You're thinking Goody Goodneck could have set someone after ye?"

"It's possible. She's rather vindictive and unforgiving."

"Like snuggling a porcupine, eh? What was the bad news ye gave her?"

"That Brighid would not give succor or aid to the damned Puritans."

"Hold on, now. They petitioned her to intervene in the damnation? When she's not even a deity of their faith?"

"They probably calculated that since they were already damned, they might as well ask around. This is something that happens often, but of course no god would go pick a fight with another by effectively stealing souls. It's just complaining."

"I had no idea such things went on. How do they even get to talk to ye?"

"Sometimes they offer tantalizing scraps of information. Goody Goodneck claimed to have something of interest but that proved to be a lie."

"How often is your time wasted on things like this? Or Brighid's?"

"Depressingly often."

"So what did Goody Goodneck say when ye gave her the news?"

"Ahem. Well. She said my stones would shrivel and I would rue the day I crossed her."

"And yer stones…?"

"Display no visible shrinkage, thank you for asking."

"So what power does she have then, to come after ye?"

Coriander shrugged. "None that I know of."

"We can cross her off then. Who else?"

"None of the Goblin Lords like me."

"Do they like anybody, though?"

"No, but they especially dislike me."

"That's a possibility then. Who else?"

"A few trolls."

"Bah. They're not smart enough to pull off something like this. It would require thinking."

"Agreed."

I looked back up at Slomo dangling from the tree branch above. *Still smell spicy up there?*

<Yes.>

Slomo, maybe the smell is coming from the tree, not the ground.

<Whoa, Oaken! That's a thing that could be true! How do we find out?>

Can ye move down the branch and see if the smell gets any stronger? I'll give ye some extra energy to burn.

Providing Slomo the energy to burn was necessary if I wanted anything to happen quickly. She'd take an hour to move otherwise.

<Ha haaaa!> Slomo crowed as the energy arrived in her system. <It's like a bunch of yellow tube fuel all at once!> That's what she called bananas. I secretly wanted to replace the BANANA signs in my local grocery with YELLOW TUBE FUEL in her honor.

Slomo scooted further along the branch and abruptly halted. <Pffauggh! It's really spicy here! Plus there are grooves in the branch and something sticky. This First Dangle is not the best, Oaken. If all the trees in Spain are like this we should probably visit somewhere else.>

They're not all like this one, love, I promise. Ye may have found a clue for us though. Why don't ye go back or even hop to another branch and I'll check it out.

<Okay, Oaken, I like that plan.> She began to move back to the trunk while I stripped off me clothes.

"What are you doing?" Coriander asked. People always ask that when you take off your clothes and I don't know why. Isn't it obvious?

"Going to check out that thick branch above us," I said, pointing up. "Slomo says there's something odd about it. Ye have your own wings, don't ye? Take a look with me if ye want."

"That's all right. I'll wait for your assessment."

With me clothes off and piled safely away from the mess, I bound me shape to that of a red kite, my avian form, and flew up to the branch to have a look.

Becoming a kite is me second favorite form after the bear. It's such a different perspective from the human one and methinks it's healthy to step outside of one's accustomed view and look at the world through different lenses.

<Hey Oaken?>

<Yes?>

<What happens to the tiny snake that lives in the fur between your legs when you shape-shift to a bird? I worry about him.>

<I told you that wasn't a snake!>

<Is it a worm or a grub or something?>

<It's part of my body, that's all.>

<Does it eat frogs and mice like snakes do and then go to sleep for a week?>

<No, but that's going to be featured in me nightmares now, so thanks for that. Okay, let's focus here. I see the grooves you were talking about. Those were made by sharp claws.>

<But not mine!>

<No. There's some slime or gunk or something and I'm not sure I smell anything in particular. Kites don't smell very well. But there are scorch marks here too. In a pattern. This is a binding. A hook binding if I'm not mistaken.>

<What's that?>

<It's a trap. A summoning spell that triggers when conditions are met. Think about how a spider's web works. Bug flies in the web and it summons the spider, right?>

<Most of the time. Sometimes the spiders just hide in the yellow tube fuel and jump at the monkeys. I saw one do that once.>

<There was a spider in the bananas big enough to eat a monkey?>

<Yeah. Happens all the time, the trees say.>

<More nightmares for me! Thanks. Anyway, someone pulled a demon here, and that's what you're smelling, no doubt. I've gotta tell Coriander. Excuse me.>

I dropped down to me clothes and shifted back to human.

<Yay! The tiny snake is back!>

Still not a snake!

<Does it have a name?>

There are lots of names for that body part, but I haven't given it a name meself.

<Can I give it a name? A Slothian name?>

Sure, go ahead.

<I will call the tiny snake Bonosamococo!>

And we can call it Bono for short?

<Sure!>

Heh. That's surprisingly close to one of the human names for it.

"Well?" Coriander demanded as I dressed. "What did you see?"

"There's a hook binding on the branch to summon a demon when humans stand underneath it. The demon's claw raked through the bits that would have told me what it was. Also destroyed the binding so there won't be any more coming, so that's good, at least. But you see the problem."

"How did anyone know Maria and Javier would be here?"

"Exactly. So how did you set up this rendezvous?"

"At our last meeting. In London."

"In the privacy of your hotel room?"

"No, we were in the Royal Botanical Gardens at Kew, lounging under a similar tree and remarking on how lovely it was, but rather lacking in privacy. People all around."

"Close enough to hear?"

"Yes, though it didn't appear anyone was listening intently."

"Appearances aside…ye gave them explicit instruction on how to find this place at that time, and no other?"

"Yes. So…that must have been it. But the humans nearby— well. I didn't sense any ill intent from them."

"It didn't need to be a human nearby, did it?"

"What do you mean?"

"Did you look up in the tree?" I pointed at Slomo and made sure she understood what I was saying to Coriander. "You never know what could be hanging around in one of those."

<Sloths!> Slomo said. <Lizards! Mantises! Monkeys! Even toucans! Evil, nasty toucans, with their dead, soulless eyes!>

Coriander considered Slomo and how quietly she was dangling there. He paled. "No. I guess it could have been the Fae."

"Sure. A pixie or somethin' could have been eavesdroppin' up there. And it could have been something or someone else. We don't know, and we need to, right? Or are ye satisfied that it was a demon and we should just leave it alone?"

"No, I want to know who's responsible and…what happened to the demon?"

"I can check with the elemental and see if it can be sensed. But my guess is that it's a flier or we would have seen some tracks. Only evidence we've found is in the tree."

"So it's just…flying around?"

"Unless whoever summoned it took care to send it back, yes. That's honestly not my worry. A runaway demon is something we can hand off to Granuaile. But finding out who's behind it is a much bigger deal. So: Can ye remember which tree ye sat under at the Kew Gardens?"

"Yes. It was near the Glass House."

"I presume there's a bound tree there we can use."

"Indubitably."

"Well then, let's away to London."

CHAPTER 3

The Kew Gardens are beautiful grounds, a testament to what people can do without any Druids to help them. If they'd thought to take such care with the rest of the planet, maybe Gaia wouldn't be so fecked up with pollution. But I think people who give a damn about the planet aren't the ones in power for some reason. I suspect the reason might be money.

Near a huge structure called the Glass House—presumably the place whence people should never throw stones—an oak tree of two hundred years or so spread out its branches over a mulched canopy. People in linens and sunglasses and tropical flower prints strolled or sprawled nearby, but no one noticed us appear. At first, anyway. Once Slomo started retching on me shoulder, heads turned in our direction, and people said things like "What the hell is that?" but then they gasped and said, "Oh my God, it's a sloth!" and started to jog or bounce or flail in our direction.

Time to dangle unless ye want to be pawed by a bunch of strangers, I said.

Slomo's answer edged toward panic. <Oh, no, Oaken, get me dangling now please!>

I lifted her up to the oak tree and boosted her so she could reach the lowest branch and hoist herself out of harm's way, and then planted myself in front of the trunk so no one could get to her without going through me first.

Hold still and dangle. I'm going to make ye disappear.

<I call First Dangle in this place! Where are we again?>

England. I cast camouflage on her and she melted from view, human eyes unable to distinguish her from the tree and surroundings.

<That tickles,> Slomo giggled. <So what is this place famous for?>

Colonialism, Shakespeare, and a fictional detective named Sherlock Holmes.

<Aren't we detectives now?> Slomo asked, ignoring the other things.

I suppose we are. Maybe we'll score ourselves a show on TV.

A trio of people, breathless with excitement, arrived to get a better look at the sloth. It was two teenaged girls and a man who was probably the father of one of them, if not both.

"Ohmigod you have a *sloth*? How did you *get* one? I want one!" the first girl said.

"Where did it go?" asked the other.

"It was so cute, I want to squeeze it!" the first one added, looking up at the tree branches.

There was no helping it; the best way to get rid of them fast was to be rude.

"There's no sloth. Go away," I said.

"But we saw one," the first teenager protested.

"No ye didn't. These are gardens, not a zoo. Me friend and I want to discuss tree parasites. Go away."

"Look here, there's no need to be so insufferably Irish," the man said.

"I think ye could stand a whole lot more suffering, lad. Away with ye now or I'll give ye some for free."

"Are you threatening me?" he challenged, his face reddening.

"Yes." I pulled out me brass knuckles and slipped them on. He paled quickly. "Go away or I turn your face into marmalade."

"I'm reporting you to security," he said, already herding the teens away.

"You do that."

Once they were gone I dropped Slomo's camouflage. *Sorry about that, love. This is a public place and you're adorable so humans are gonna react like that whenever they see you.*

<They made lots of noises. What was that about?>

They wanted to pet you and I told them to leave. Smell anything weird up there? Spicy or anything?

<No.>

Coriander sighed. "This was weeks ago. There probably aren't any clues remaining even if any were left at the time."

"Only one way to find out." I cast camouflage on meself and stripped again. "Stand guard here, will ye? I imagine some security types might show up soon but ye can handle them, right?"

"They will handle themselves, yes."

I chuckled. "I'll try to be quick."

"No, please, take all the time you need."

I bound me form to a kite, flew up into the tree above Slomo, and dropped the camouflage.

<Hey, Oaken! You're a bird again!>

<That's right. Looking for clues.>

<What do clues look like? Maybe I can help you look for some.>

<Anything out of the ordinary. Something up in the tree that doesn't belong.>

<Do little soft things that aren't tree bark belong?>

<Maybe not. Where's that?>

<Under my claws I think. Feels pretty welcoming for a tree, I thought, but maybe that's just England.>

I hopped over to where Slomo was dangling and sure enough, a small pink cloth was underneath her claws and caught on a sharp piece of bark. I teased it out with my beak, pinned it underneath me talons, and examined it.

<Huh. This is a perfect square.>

<Is that a clue?>

<Maybe so. This isn't a torn piece of cloth. It was made this way. It's sewn. Even has a little monogram on it, so that's a clue to who owns it. But it's tiny for a handkerchief. Might not be a human's.>

<Who else would put their initials on a piece of cloth? Not sloths! Maybe a capybara would though. They're very fancy and polite and all the other animals love them.>

<Faeries might. Even pixies. Though the more I look at it, the more I think this wasn't intended to be a handkerchief at all. It has stains on it. Food stains, I mean.>

<So they used it as a napkin?>

<No. I think they carried food in it and had it tied up with string. This could have carried a picnic lunch for a pixie. They sat up here and eavesdropped on Coriander. And then something happened to make them leave this behind.>

<Like what?>

<I don't know. It would be speculation. But I don't think they'd leave this behind for us to find weeks later without a reason. We'll see if Coriander recognizes it.>

I dropped down to the ground to give Coriander the cloth and shifted to human once I got there. "Here," I said. "Found this. Recognize it?"

Coriander took it and frowned, but before he could answer I heard some gasps and exclamations nearby and realized that in my excitement I'd forgotten what era we were in. People thought nudity remarkable now so they were remarking on mine.

"Look, there he is!" someone shouted. It was the man who'd threatened to fetch security earlier, and he had followed through. He had a large bloke with him and he was pointing at me, loudly proclaiming that I was not only prone to violence but to perversion. "He's a menace!"

"Well, time to go," I said. "Come on, Slomo, drop down and I'll catch ye."

"I recognize this," Coriander said, frowning down at the pink scrap.

"Tell me later," I urged him. "We need to talk elsewhere." Slomo dropped down from the branch and I swung her around to me back.

<Whoa-ho! What a ride!>

Her claws scratched me up but there was no helping it. Security was sprinting toward me and shouting at me to get down on the ground. I scooped up me clothes giving them a prize view of me backside, and then the streaking began.

The patrons of the Royal Gardens got a superb value for their ticket price that day, seeing a naked man with a sloth on his back running in tandem with someone who looked like a movie star away from an outmatched security guard. We could have bested him in combat if we wished but that would only have drawn more attention. We were headed to a copse of trees and could easily lose him in there.

"I'm going to cast camouflage—" I began.

"No, don't bother," Coriander said. "There's an Old Way to Tír na nÓg here."

"Do we want to go there?"

"Yes. We do."

I was asking more for Slomo's benefit than mine. She'd just had herself a fine yak and was probably feeling a bit weak. It was too soon to shift planes again. But maybe traveling via an Old Way—a convoluted path through the forest that would bridge the planes—wouldn't have the same effect on her as using tethered trees.

Sometimes humans stumbled across these paths, slipped into Tír na nÓg, and were never seen again. It wasn't common but it could happen.

We ducked behind a hedge, temporarily out of sight, and then Coriander took the lead and I followed directly behind him. We wove through bushes in a sinuous pattern and they weren't the sort that completely shielded us from view, so the security guard located us again and took a much straighter path through them than we did.

"Coriander, lad, I don't mean to rush ye," I said after taking a quick glance over me shoulder, "but how long is this Old Way?" I was worried what the guard might to do Slomo if he tried to tackle us.

"Almost there," the faery replied, and he was as good as his word. The huffing and puffing of the guard faded, as did the ambient noise of Kew Gardens, and the plants changed and the sound of the birds did too as our footsteps took us into Tír na nÓg. To the security guard's eyes, we would have gone transparent before fading from view. I hoped he'd be smart about it and say he just lost us.

<Whoa, that was quite a chase scene, Oaken! Birds will do that in the trees sometimes, complete with the shouting and everything, but I never know what gets them that way. Say… why did we run?>

Other people wouldn't let us find clues in peace.

<But we found one anyway!>

Yes we did. And thank you for your assistance.

<This thing we are doing is very strange, if you don't mind me saying.>

Of course I don't mind. You can say what ye like. I want to hear it. What's so strange?

<Well, when we find a monkey or a snake or a frog dead in the jungle, no one ever tries to find out who did it. I mean, it

was probably the toucans, because it's always the toucans, but nobody ever tries to find out for sure. Probably because we all know it was the toucans. What do you do when you find out who did it?>

We try to hold them accountable. Bring them to justice. Make them pay, somehow, for the crime.

<Wait. Are you saying we could have been bringing toucans to justice *this whole time?*>

I guess so. You'd have to set up a judicial system with lawyers and judges and—well, no, never mind. All ye need is me. If a toucan ever bothers ye, Slomo, I'll punch it right in the beak.

<Wow, thanks Oaken!>

Coriander halted and tuned to me, waving the cloth like some foul bumrag as I helped Slomo attach herself to a tree. She'd suffered no nausea from the trip, I noticed. I'd have to see about using Old Ways to travel with her as much as possible. Maybe we could even make a new one that led to her patch of rainforest in Peru.

"This kerchief," Coriander said, "belongs to a rather odious pixie who is less than friendly with Brighid and myself. She was loyal to Fand."

So it *was* a kerchief.

"But Fand is dead now," I said, "so who are pixies like her looking to these days?"

"I don't know," Coriander admitted.

"Okay, we have two branches to follow here," I said. "First, was it the pixie who left that kerchief there and eavesdropped on your conversation, or was it someone else who wanted to frame the pixie?"

"Oh," Coriander said, blinking in surprise. He hadn't thought of the second possibility.

"Second, if it's the pixie, could they have set that hook binding by themselves?"

"No. Certainly not."

"So that would imply the pixie is working for someone more powerful. And maybe there are factions involved here—I'm just thinkin' aloud, ye understand, because I think something must have made that pixie leave in a hurry."

"Why is that?"

"Because it's an obvious clue that will lead us directly to them. Only reason they'd leave it behind is because they had no choice, or it's a frame job. So is there a faction or two in Court that would object to that pixie eavesdropping on ye?"

"For certain. Those who are loyal to Brighid."

"So ye mean someone on your side might be running counter-intelligence ops?"

"Yes."

"If that's the case, then, why didn't we hear anything about this?"

"I've been away from Court. Perhaps Brighid knows something. She may have tried to warn me. I wouldn't know."

"What's a better bet, finding the owner of this kerchief, or finding out more from Court?"

"Court, without a doubt. I have no idea where to begin looking for the pixie anyway, except at Court."

"Can we get there without shifting? Me sloth doesn't handle it well."

"We can. Follow me."

There were shortcuts built into Tír na nÓg much like Old Ways that we could travel with Coriander escorting us. It wasn't long until we were breaking into the dense copse of trees that ringed the large meadow of Faery Court.

And there, waiting for us with triple flails in hand, was a pack of kilted badger men.

CHAPTER 4

On the one hand, I'll always love and respect the Dagda for his creative energy and his vital role in making sure the Fae kept the Tuatha Dé Danann powerful and relevant to humans. The sheer breadth of his voluminous seed ensured that the magic of the Fae—the magic of Druids—would never truly disappear from the earth. And it had resulted in truly remarkable wonders like unicorns and merfolk.

On the other hand, he was also responsible for trolls and goblins and all manner of ornery critters because he couldn't stop copulating with any hole-shaped orifice he found.

Badger folk were created when he fecked a badger den one day—not the actual badgers, mind, but the whole bloody den, because it was a hole in the ground that he found inviting, or winsome somehow, and nothing would do until he had humped it urgently and deposited a quick cocksplat into its depths. His incredibly potent package thereby created badger men who adopted the dress of Scots and played the most miserable bagpipes in the planes. Disagreeable types, in other words, who looked ready to disagree with our intention to proceed.

"Ackphth," one of them spat. "Rapth nak spuffthuk hurrrrk."

"Don't mumble, now, lads. Be plain and use your words."

And then they attacked us, because badgers are like that, and we'd already received more courtesy than we could reasonably expect, and the day a badger uses words instead of claws is the day a fish stops breathing in water.

They were quick and savage and Coriander stepped in front of us to take the first assault while I slipped on me brass knuckles. Crafted by Creidhne, they allowed me to punch through most anything. I could take on a wall of granite and the stone would come out the worse for it. But me powerful offense is nothing compared to Coriander's defenses.

He's surrounded by kinetic wards that reflect a hunnert-fifty to two hunnert percent of the force directed against him. So punch if ye like, he'll let ye, but in the meantime your bones will be shattered and you'll be knocked backwards besides. Fire a gun at him and the bullet will come screaming back to destroy your spleen. Whip a flail at him, as one of the badger men did, and you'll find the spiked balls of it embedded in your skull double-quick.

The second badger man, seeing the first go down with his own weapon and Coriander unharmed, paused and blinked.

"Rraphth kackthpf?" he said.

The third badger man had either missed it, or was profoundly unable to learn from the mistakes of others. He stepped up and whipped his flail at my head from the side. I ducked underneath the swing and applied me knuckles to his knee. He went down howling over a shattered kneecap and I rose to me feet and pointed at him as I said to the second badger, "Kackthpf."

I don't know what that meant, or even if I said it correctly, but he got the message. With one comrade toast and the other disabled while we weren't wounded or even breathing hard, he realized he was confronting a class of opponent several levels above his own.

"Away with ye now, and we won't have any more blood. How would that be?"

"Poomphth," he said, and scarpered off. That left a clear path to Court, where Coriander might be able to find out what happened to the pixie who owned the handkerchief.

<Oaken, what were those angry spitting things?>

An object lesson on the dubious wisdom and provenance of fertility gods. Orgies have consequences, love.

<What's an orgy? These mental pictures are confusing.>

They tend to be sticky. You wouldn't like them.

Coriander led us to Court where a veritable swarm of Fae were working on a new throne for Brighid—one that wasn't made of iron but which made much to-do about her power and glory and such. It was largely made of living wood—boughs with mushrooms and ivy growing on it, and an appropriate cloud of butterflies and bees attending it all.

Brighid sat off to one side in the meantime and looked quite surprised to see her Herald Extraordinary in his workaday duds.

"Coriander? And Eoghan? What news?"

He drew her aside to speak for a while in privacy and I got to answer Slomo's questions about the Fae.

<Lots of them fly but they're not birds?>

That's right.

<So no relation to toucans?>

Not even a little.

<Are any of them like mantises that eat your head if they get a chance?>

Some of them might do that, but they're not like mantises. Most of the Fae eat leaves and flowers like you. But occasionally they eat the hearts of children. You can't be too careful around the Fae. They're like humans in that regard. They could be completely lovely and they could be the most depraved monsters of your nightmares. Approach them with caution.

<That's an important safety tip. Saaaaay, who are those people over there that have arm markings like yours?>

Over where? Oh. Them.

It took me a moment to see who Slomo meant because there was such a muddled cluster of creatures milling about the meadow of the Fae Court, but it turned out she was looking at a small, radiant group of the Tuatha Dé Danann who all had the same Druidic tattoos on their arms as I did. They glowed faintly, being fecking awesome and knowing it, and they were surrounded by a cluster of attendant faeries.

Those are very powerful beings, I said to her. *Goddesses of the Irish, like Brighid.*

<When you say powerful, what do you mean by that? Can they just walk up to a toucan and shut them down and say NO DEADLY TOUCAN GAMES TODAY, or what?>

Fecking hells, love, you really have a problem with big-beaked birds. They could indeed do that if they wished, but I can practically guarantee you that they are not interested in toucans.

<Then what are they interested in?>

Power, mostly. Who has it, and who doesn't, and how much. Though I'm not sure it really matters to them; it is more of a game they play because if they don't, they'll die of boredom.

<Can you die of boredom?>

Indirectly, yes. Boredom makes you do stupid things to entertain yourself and sometimes those things are fatal. Like parkour.

<Whoa, those humans are trying to do monkey stunts and failing!> Slomo said, responding to the images I sent.

Right? Kids these days.

<So who are the goddesses?>

I nodded faintly at the nearest one, since pointing was likely to be taken as an insult. She was a regal looking dark-haired woman in modest white robes and a crown of white roses ringing her head. She was attended by several fairies in similar garb.

That one is Ecne, goddess of wisdom. She's the daughter of three brothers and therefore tends to call everyone uncle.

<Is that normal for humans?>

Not really. It's called fraternal polyandry and it's also sticky. See the next three to her left?

I indicated a trio of ethereal beauties, each of them coolly watching Brighid speak with Coriander without seeming to be particularly interested. One was blonde, another brunette, and the third red-haired. They had a small horde of faeries flitting about them, waiting to do whatever their laconic natures might desire.

That's Eriu, Banba, and Fodhla, the patron goddesses of Ireland.

<They look like they say fancy words and eat fancy things.>

Artisanal toast for sure, I agreed. *And they can sling a fine poem when they feel like it.*

<And who's that off to the side? She looks ready to fight.> Slomo stretched a discreet claw toward a woman who looked anything but bored by the construction of Brighid's throne. Disgusted or contemptuous, more likely. She had her dark hair gathered into a queue and ringed in gold hoops, and she plainly wore armor and weapons in contrast to the other Tuatha Dé Danann.

That's because she always is. That's Clíodhna, the Queen of the Banshees. The bean sídhe, I should say. That's them floating behind her, the Fae in gray flying without wings.

They were only two or three feet high, ragged gray cloaks draped over wizened, wrinkled frames dressed in diaphanous green. Their eyes glowed red and their white hair swirled around their heads like thunderclouds. They moved slowly but constantly in a gentle churn of movement behind their leader.

<What do the bean sídhe do?>

They are harbingers of death. I hear they were supremely annoyed at being left behind when the Fae host went to fight in Ragnarok. They missed a lot of quality keening and wailing that day. But Clíodhna was particularly unhappy to miss out on the slaughter. She's been itching for one.

<That armor does look a bit itchy.>

Now that I think of it, when it comes to death and who might have died recently among the Fae, the bean sídhe might have some answers for us. Let's go have a chat.

<What if she starts a fight with us?>

Oh, she'd never do that, love. Unless she feels like it.

CHAPTER 5

I took three whole steps toward Clíodhna before Coriander broke away from Brighid and floated my way, indicating he'd like a word.

"The pixie in question was indeed, as I suspected, loyal to Fand rather than Brighid," Coriander said. "Like many such Fae, she worked in service to one of the other Tuatha Dé Danann rather than work for Brighid directly. But Brighid hasn't seen her at Court for weeks, which corresponds to my picnic in Kew Gardens. It's likely the pixie hasn't returned to Tír na nÓg, or if she has, she's been very careful not to attend Court."

I gave the barest nod toward the Queen of the Banshees. "I was about to ask Clíodhna if she might know whether that pixie was still around or not."

Coriander's eyes darted that way briefly and returned to mine. "She does not give such information away for free."

"Ah. Well, never mind then." The last thing I'd ever do is get myself in debt to the Tuatha Dé Danann. That kind of dealing is what got Siodhachan in so much trouble.

"No, it is a good idea. I will pay whatever she wishes. It's not normal for the pixie to be absent this long. Something has happened."

The Herald Extraordinary led the way and the cluster of goddesses and faeries shifted subtly at his approach. Clíodhna crossed her arms in front of her, a clear negative signal. Soon after, Fodhla and Banba mirrored this. They were all but shouting that they did not welcome him, either personally or as a herald of the First among the Fae. It looked like some of them were curious about my presence here, which I did not appreciate. Drawing the attention of the Fae rarely worked out to one's benefit. It was best to live in such a way that they never knew of your existence, or failing that, in such a way that they found uninteresting.

Coriander and Clíodhna exchanged stilted formal greetings and then the herald asked about the pixie.

"I know what happened to her, yes," the queen said. "But there is a price for such information."

"I will deliver a written message for you to any lesser being on any of the planes so long as it does not conflict in any way with my duties for Brighid; if it does, the priorities and wishes of the First among the Fae must supersede yours."

Clíodhna raised an eyebrow. "Good enough. It is a bargain. Know then that the pixie in question is dead. The bean sídhe wailed for her."

"When?"

"Two weeks past."

"How did she die?"

"Violently. But the precise manner of it was shrouded from our sight."

"Where?"

Clíodhna shrugs. "Somewhere on the mortal plane. But there is nothing to find or investigate. She was finished off with iron. That is why we know so little."

Coriander's shoulders drooped. "Very well. Good day."

I noticed that the Tuatha Dé Danann were pleased to see him defeated. They uncrossed their arms and their mouths upturned in smug smiles of victory. They might simply be happy about his unhappiness, or they might be behind it all. Any or all of them could bear a grudge against Brighid and Coriander, and I wouldn't know without prying further than I should.

We stepped back out of earshot and Coriander looked a bit desolate.

"That was our only clue. And it's led us to a literal dead end."

"Not necessarily, lad. We can still eliminate options. Was it someone on Brighid's side who went after that pixie or someone against her who was covering their tracks?"

"Not anyone on Brighid's side. She would know."

"Right. So someone was covering their tracks."

"But we have no idea who that might be."

"Not yet. But it's only been a wee while since we started. It could be those Goblin Lords ye mentioned and we haven't even gone to see them yet. Give it a chance."

"I should go home to clean up and change."

"Go ahead. I'm going to chat up the goddess of wisdom and see if she has any advice."

"Good idea. I'll return soon."

He floated away, head drooping and probably doing all he could not to scream his frustration. I walked toward the scent of roses.

<Oaken, where is he going?>

He'll be back soon. I'm going to talk to this lady for a short while and then hopefully we can leave here and find a nice place to dangle.

I nodded in respect to the goddess of wisdom. "Your pardon, Ecne. May I introduce myself?"

She inclined her head the tiniest bit.

"You may."

"I am Eoghan Ó Cinneadie, a Druid in service to Gaia."

"I have heard of you. You have recently convened a grove of six apprentices, is that correct?"

"It is."

"I am glad to hear it. We need more Druids."

"I couldn't agree more. Forgive me if this seems out of turn to ask, Ecne, but might you know how to create a hook binding?"

She didn't blink or look alarmed in any way, which is what I would expect if she were guilty. Instead she smiled at me and said, "Of course. I was hired to complete one just recently."

CHAPTER 6

You could have basted my balls in butter and basil before I would have allowed you to point the finger at Ecne. I'd planned to ask her who else might know how to complete such bindings, but never thought she would readily admit to hiring herself out for such work. I could tell she wasn't joking, but felt the need to clarify in case this was some other job she was talking about.

"Was this hook binding near Granada, Spain, by any chance?"

Her easy smile evaporated. "Yes. How did you know that?"

"I saw the result. May I ask who hired you to do it?"

She shrugged, unconcerned about the extraordinarily messy deaths of two people. "I do not know who requested the contract, but the job came to me through a middle man who arranges all sorts of unusual transactions. I have done similar work for him before. He thinks of himself as a spider in the center of a web of connections, so he operates under the name Texas Weaver."

"Seriously? What a load of—"

"He also goes online twice a year and buys lube in fifty-five gallon drums," she added.

"What the—"

"And he has an orb weaver tattoo in the middle of his chest with the improper number of eyes. Poor attention to detail there on the part of the artist."

I was not going to venture a guess as to how Ecne knew about the tattoo on his chest. "So I guess you have…visited him in person."

"I have. He was able to acquire some ancient texts I wish to peruse. In return, I performed a hook binding for a demon at that specific place in Granada and agreed to banish it afterward."

"And did you banish whatever it was?"

"Yes."

That was a relief, at least. We didn't have a creature that turned people inside out roaming the planet.

"So this Texas Weaver gave no hint about why you needed to craft a hook binding at that place, or who the target was?"

"No. That was not my concern."

"It may concern you to know that the people who were killed by that demon were Coriander's lovers."

Ecne's eyes flicked around the Court, searching for the Herald Extraordinary and not finding him. Her lips pressed together in regret.

"Do you jest with me? I do not find it amusing."

"I am quite serious. Your work was a trap set for his paramours."

"That is very disappointing news. I would not willingly give him offense."

"He's extremely upset. He asked me to help him track down who did it. It's why I'm here."

Her eyes returned to me, guarded now. "Well done, then, Druid. But I was not targeting him or his lovers. I merely performed a binding in exchange for services rendered."

"There's nothing you can tell me about the client?"

A bare shake of the head. "No. You will have to extract that information from the Texas Weaver. That will not be easy. He is careful to protect his clients' privacy."

"It's worth a try."

The eyes softened and a faint hint of amusement played about Ecne's lips. "Indeed. You may find him at The White Horse in Austin, Texas."

"The White Horse?"

"Yes. Tragically, it contains no actual horses of any color. It is a specific variety of establishment that the mortals call a honky tonk bar. While inside, they consume alcohol and clomp around in boots and hats to live music that I find about as soothing as the howling of cats."

"A perfect description of all modern music, if I may say so. How will I know this Texas Weaver?"

"You cannot miss him. He also has spider tattoos up the length of both arms, and he always has glamoured muscle standing nearby."

"Fae muscle, ye mean? What kind?"

"The deadly kind, but stuffed into cowboy boots. It must be seen to be believed."

"How quickly can I get there from here?"

"There's an Old Way to the Texas State Cemetery, which is located a short distance from the site. I made it myself since I have frequent cause to go there. Because I have trespassed against the herald's goodwill, I will lead you that far."

CHAPTER 7

I noted with a mixture of amusement and dread that Ecne utterly failed to inform Coriander when he returned that she had created the hook binding that killed Maria and Javier Garces. She stressed instead that she was taking us to Austin to confront the Texas Weaver who could tell us, with sufficient persuasion, who had requested the hit.

Coriander didn't look quite so fabulous anymore. Or I suppose he'd opted for a different sort of fabulous. He had put on a poet's shirt and some black leather pants, teased his hair, and applied several layers of black makeup around the hollows of his eyes. His black boots had buckles and straps on the sides plus chunky heels, but he still didn't quite touch the ground. He was goth or emo now—I wasn't sure which, but I figured the distinction was something people could argue about on the Internet and it wouldn't really matter except to people who were goth or emo and wanted to be seen as one but not the other. What mattered to me was that his soulful eyes invited you in to share his pain, and I thought it was a simply fantastic choice for mourning the loss of loved ones but might draw some double takes in an Austin honky tonk. But then again, the Peruvian sloth clinging to me back was probably going to get a few stares as well. We were going in anyway.

I appreciated taking the Old Way so that Slomo's digestion wouldn't take a hit. Her belly grumbled as we moved.

Hungry, love?

<Yes, very hungry. It has been an exciting day.>

We'll see if we can get ye something ahead here.

We were in a much later time zone when we got to Texas and the White Horse wouldn't be open for a while. We had some time to kill so I let Slomo dangle from a tree in the cemetery—a nicely sprawling property of manicured grass and stone—and she discovered its leaves were quite delicious.

Ecne left us there and casually mentioned to me that I could tell Coriander who made the hook binding as she walked back along the Old Way and disappeared.

"What? You know who did it?" Coriander's teeth clenched. "How long have you known?"

"About twenty minutes. Since just before you returned looking like a tragic vampire. Listen, who did it and who ordered it are two different things, wouldn't you agree?"

"Tell me who did it!"

"Who ordered it, you mean? Because that's who you want. You know very well that you can make a hook binding and leave and never know who's going to trigger it."

Coriander closed his eyes and took a deep breath. He let it out slowly before continuing in calmer tones. "Of course I wish to know both. And I am aware of the difference. Now tell me who did it."

I hooked a thumb in the direction of the recently departed goddess. "It was Ecne."

The herald's eyes popped. "Ecne!"

"Yeah. Funny how she forgot to mention it, isn't it? I can't tell you whether her story is truth or not, but this business with the Weaver—she said he set it all up. He hired her for a binding and that's it. She claims she did it in exchange for some ancient books and had no idea about the target."

Coriander's fists clenched and his pale face turned blotchy and red and he shook with rage.

<Is that guy gonna explode, Oaken?>

Maybe.

But he didn't. He quivered quite a bit and took huge sucking breaths to calm down, but he eventually went still as one of the tombstones. When he spoke it was calm and measured.

"You realize we could be walking into a trap."

"I do. And dying in a honky tonk is not the way I want to go. I'll stick around to help ye find out who did this. But getting revenge, lad? That's your business."

"I appreciate that."

I relaxed under Slomo's branch while Coriander wandered aimlessly among the tombstones, looking like he was there to shoot a music video. The weather was all wrong for it, though, bright and sunny. He needed some proper thunderclouds. I toyed with the idea of pulling in a small cloud of water vapor to follow him around, but that would have been a frivolous use of power.

<Hey, you know what, Oaken?>

What's that, love?

<These leaves are pretty tasty and there aren't any monkeys or toucans to bother me. I like dangling here.>

Good. I'm glad we are having a wee while to enjoy being here. It's a fulfilling exercise, ye know.

<What is?>

Being conscious of how good it is to be here right now. Too often we get so busy with our little problems we forget how wonderful it is to be alive. I'm not supposed to be here, really, in this time and place. I was supposed to die two thousand years ago. So as fecking hellish as this paved-over world can be sometimes, I am grateful to be here. There's a werewolf in Arizona who loves me. Apprentices who trust me. Friends like you. And there's plenty of good work to fill my days. All of this is good.

<I agree, Oaken! But I am not sure the other guy would.>

No, he wouldn't. Right now he's thinking of how bad everything is. He's in mourning. He's lost people he loves and it's a hole in his life he can't think how to fill right now. He wants to fill that hole with vengeance, but that's not really filling. It's hollow.

<Sort of like leaves that are mostly water?>

Sort of, yeah.

Once the sun kissed the horizon with a blazing yellow smooch, we exited the cemetery and walked the couple of blocks down Comal St. to the White Horse. It was a flat-roofed building with a fenced-in patio area containing an orange taco truck with BOMB TACOS emblazoned on the side. I paused outside to draw some energy from the earth and fill the reservoirs in me brass knuckles. I used some of it right away to cast camouflage on Slomo so that she wouldn't cause comment when we walked in. Lots of places have laws against animals in a drinking establishment, presumably because they weren't going to buy a round.

Our entrance caused heads to turn and the needle might have scratched right off the vinyl of an old album if they had such a system. But they had a digital jukebox that kept playing unperturbed since the band wasn't playing yet, a man moaning about all the whiskey he drank because of his cheatin' woman.

I grinned because I knew we looked like alien creatures to this particular clientele. Coriander, in particular, didn't fit in. I think maybe he was wearing the wrong sort of boots. At least I had jeans on.

First thing we saw was a pool table just to the right of the door with a lamp dangling over it, yellow squares of light that gave way to stained glass renditions of fruit at the bottom. The impression was that they had grown out of the fertile soil of the table's green felt. The two dudes playing looked up from their game and scowled, trying to place us in their paradigm and rapidly coming to the conclusion that we were outside of it.

There were six tables clustered beyond the pool table with chairs, about half occupied at the moment, but they could easily be moved out whenever they needed more room for dancing. Past that was the stage set in the corner, its walls sheathed in red curtains and lights shining down on a drum kit and microphone stands, promising a good time later. I thought it would probably be a fun place to bring Greta and she could teach me how to two-step. Or if she didn't know how, we'd learn together.

Opposite that was an expansive bar with various beers and liquors advertised in neon. About half the stools there were occupied already because the Happy Hour was much longer than a single hour and it was cheap, according to a chalkboard with the specials listed.

Gesturing to Coriander that he should follow me, I led the way to the bar because we had to look like we were there for fun or, if that wasn't believable, hoping to get some directions since we were so obviously lost.

I kept my eyes moving for threat assessment but no one looked particularly annoyed at us being there. They were mostly confused and maybe wondering if we were there to start some shite. Well, I didn't want to start anything, particularly. But I was prepared to finish whatever did get started.

<Owen, what's that noise?> Slomo asked.

Country music.

<Is it going to stop?>

Not in Texas, love. I know it's kind of loud, but hopefully we won't have to stay here very long.

<The human sounds like he is in pain.>

He is. Sometimes unhealthy relationships make humans sad and they write songs about it. They write songs about healthy relationships too, I think. But they're not as popular for some reason. Maybe because people empathize with unhealthy relationships more.

The bartender had a sprinkling of stubble on his face and a sleeve tattoo. He noted my tattoo briefly and chucked his chin at me. "What can I get you?"

I scanned the Happy Hour menu and asked for two shots of tequila, which Siodhachan had told me was powerful stuff. I'd never had tequila before, and I was willing to bet Coriander hadn't either. I put down ten dollars on the bar because they were four dollars apiece and Greta explained to me that ye have to give servers more money than the price of the food in America because of capitalism.

The shots got poured quickly into small glasses, served with a lime wedge on the rim, and strangely, very pointedly, with a salt shaker. That puzzled Coriander too.

"I am familiar with the human fondness for shots of alcohol, but why did he provide us with salt and citrus?" he asked.

"I don't know."

"What if there is a ritual associated with these items and we perform it improperly, thereby giving offense?"

"Good point. We should ask."

I turned to a man to my right who was already staring at us with his mouth open, which meant I wouldn't need to get his attention. He was wearing a simple black T-shirt and jeans with a giant silver buckle.

"I've never done a tequila shot before. Is there some specific way I'm supposed to do it?"

"Where you from, dude?" he asked, which didn't answer my question. "England?"

"Feck no. I'm from Ireland."

"What's wrong with England?"

"It's not Ireland."

"Huh huh." He found that amusing and gave me a half grin. "Texas ain't Ireland either."

"I agree."

"So that means Texas and England are exactly the same?"

"Exactly the same as far as I'm concerned."

"Hee! You're funny. All right, dude, shake some salt onto your hand in between the thumb and forefinger. Yeah. Like that. Get yer buddy set up too. Right. Now whatcha gotta do is a 1-2-3 operation. You lick the salt offa your hand, gulp the shot, then bite into the lime wedge and suck on it."

"Why?"

"Some folks find that tequila can be a bit harsh, and they think the salt and lime cut down on that somehow."

Shrugging and checking with Coriander to make sure he was still game, the Herald Extraordinary gave a nod and we did the lick, shot, and suck sequence.

Tequila, for the record, does not go down like whiskey.

I coughed a couple times, but Coriander did a bit of a flop and twitch as he gasped and hacked.

"Whyyy?" he rasped in a hoarse whisper.

The guy who told us what to do was having a pretty good laugh about it, and some others joined in. That was all right. They liked us for being so willing to publicly humiliate ourselves. Maybe we'd get out of here without any violence at all.

<I don't have to drink whatever you just drank, right Oaken?>

No, Slomo, I love ye too much to ever give ye tequila.

<Sometimes I try new leaves because I see other animals eating them and have a reaction like that.>

We all have different tastes, that's for sure. And it's okay. I am very happy for all the people who like tequila. They can have mine.

I ordered three beers and gave one to the laughing man to show there was no hard feelings, and taught him to say "Sláinte" instead of "Cheers." Then I quietly told Coriander that he should start looking for Fae in glamour. He nodded and I turned back to the man, asking his name and what other terrible shite Texas had that could set an Irishman's throat on fire.

His name was Jimmy, and he was only too happy to tell me all the things. He ordered me a shot called Dragon's Spit, which was cinnamon whiskey with ten drops of Tabasco in it, and watched with unbridled glee as I downed it and gasped afterward, tears streaming down my face. He was laughing so hard at me he had tears in his eyes too.

Having grown up in Ireland before spices were really a thing, I often had trouble with modern spicy food. Some of it burned as much on the way out as it did on the way in.

"I think he's right over there at that table," Coriander murmured.

I didn't look. "You *think* he is?" I whispered.

"No, I am certain. He is flanked by two glamoured spriggans."

Fecking spriggans. Those things are nasty. One o' them killed Goibhniu, the god of brewing, back when Fand had her rebellion against Brighid, and I'm still mad about it. The chances of us getting out of here without violence just dropped precipitously. If Slomo wasn't with me, I would practically guarantee it.

Keeping my voice low, I asked, "How do the spriggans look to humans? I'm not going to cast magical sight."

"Tall bearded men in cowboy hats and plaid shirts. The Weaver is human, and he sits between them, clean-shaven."

"All right, let's finish our beers and keep looking a bit, but don't stare."

"Why not? The spriggans are staring at us."

"Gods below. They've already made us."

"No use waiting."

I turned to Jimmy, thanked him for the drink and the laugh, and asked him to pardon us, we had to go talk to someone. He nodded but said nothing.

Turning around, I immediately saw the table Coriander meant. Two impressively sized cowboys with black beards and glittering green eyes were staring right at us. It looked like they wouldn't move very fast, but once started, they would pound the shite out of ye. Only the last part was true. Since they were spriggans, they'd move very fast and still pound the shit out of ye.

Like badger men, spriggans were born of an amorous encounter with something the Dagda really shouldn't have messed with. I don't know if it was a living tree he humped or a fallen log, but spriggans were essentially fast-moving collections of branches with an impressive vertical leap and the ability to club a skull into shards.

Sitting in between them was a scruffy but amiable sort with a hatchet jaw, a full yellow mustache, and some sandy stubble on his cheeks. I didn't see the spider tattoos he was supposed to have on his arms because he was wearing a long-sleeved pale blue shirt. He was aware of us, but was more interested in his glass of beer and a plate of nachos.

Can ye see those two big men and the smaller man eating in between them, Slomo?

<Yeah, Oaken, I can see them.>

The two big men are not actually men. That is an illusion, a trick they're playing on your eyes.

<Why are they playing that trick?>

Because they wouldn't look human otherwise and nobody would want them in here. They're like monsters. Worse than toucans.

<Worse than—oh, wow, Oaken are we gonna fight?>

Maybe. I'm going to give ye some speed and strength, but don't attack unless I say. And don't touch the human.

<Got it.>

I slipped my hands into my pockets, pushing my fingers through the holes in my brass knuckles as Coriander hailed the man with the yellow mustache.

"Hello. Mr. Weaver? May we speak to you for a moment?"

His hand, halfway to his mouth with a nacho dripping melted cheese and sour cream, paused as he eyed us suspiciously.

"How do you know that name?" His voice was pitched a bit high, querulous, and I wasn't an expert on accents the way Siodhachan was, but his accent didn't sound quite like the others at the bar. Maybe he was from a different part of Texas originally.

"We were referred to you by Ecne of the Tuatha Dé Danann. She said you might be able to help us."

CHAPTER 8

The Texas Weaver blinked once, crammed the nacho into his mouth, then dabbed at his greasy mouth and mustache with a napkin while he chewed. His eyes slid to the tattoos on my right arm, which matched those of Ecne and the other Tuatha Dé Danann, signifiying our Druidic binding to the earth. Tossing the napkin down, he nodded a couple times. "All right. What do you need?"

"Might we go outside to talk? It's a bit loud in here."

He leaned back in his chair. "What's your name?"

"I'm Coriander."

He squinted. "You mean *the* Coriander, the herald of Brighid?"

"Yes."

"Heard o' you." He looked pointedly at the faery's attire. "Don't look like you're here on official business, if y' don't mind me sayin'."

"That's because I'm not. I'm here on a personal matter."

"Okay, Coriander. But my boys here will be joining us."

"That's fine."

"It's through them double doors back there. You'll see a room with another pool table and then a patio area. Go on, we'll be there in a minute."

We moved toward the doors and I scouted for weapons that might be used against us as we did. Mostly it was the spriggans and maybe the pool cues for the extra table bracketed in some holders against the wall. That bonus room was painted yellow and there was an old upright piano, a photo booth, and a shoe shine station in there. Through double doors we were in the fenced-off patio area and the orange taco truck was to the left. That smelled good. No doubt it's where Weaver got his nachos. It was still early enough in the evening that the patio was deserted. The customers would come flooding in at the end of the work day, which might be any minute now. But the music volume was much reduced out there, so we wouldn't have to shout or risk being overheard.

<Oh, that's better, Oaken. The music isn't so loud now.>

That's right. But we might still have a fight. The roof extended over the door a bit but as it was a flat roof, rather than sloped, it was a good place for an ace in the hole. *Hey, why don't ye jump up on the roof for a minute. In case things get excitable.* Powered by the energy I was feeding to her, she nimbly leapt off my back, hooked her claws onto the edge of the roof, and pulled herself up. Or at least that's what I heard. I didn't see much through the camouflage so I couldn't be sure how nimble it was, but it was sure faster than she moved without the boost.

<Nothing to munch on up here,> she complained.

I'll see what I can find.

"Ye know why they wanted us to go first, don't ye?" I asked Coriander while I stripped a few potted plants of their leaves.

"Why?"

"So that they can block the exit in case we need our asses kicked."

The ghost of a smile played about the herald's lips. "They don't know who they're dealing with."

"He's heard of you."

"If so, I'm sure he's also heard that he's not supposed to have spriggrans as personal bodyguards. That is expressly forbidden by multiple treaties. I'm surprised the sigil agents haven't tracked him down yet."

"Sigil agents?" I held the leaves up to Slomo and she scooped them out of my hand.

<Thanks, Oaken!>

Coriander shrugged a shoulder while I shoved my hands back into my pockets to hide my brass knuckles. "They're Brighid's solution to there not being many Druids around for a long time. They enforce treaties between the Fae and humans and other parties as well."

Before I could ask any more about them, Weaver and the spriggans arrived. As I predicted, each one took up space in the two double doors leading back into the building. Weaver stayed inside and asked from behind one of them, "So who's your friend, Coriander, with the Druidic tattoos?"

"An actual Druid."

Weaver tilted his head. "Thought there was only one."

"Your information's a bit out of date," I told him, not offering any. "But never mind me; it's Coriander who has business."

"Reckon you should get to it, then," he said.

"Very well. Ecne informed us that you acquired some rare texts for her."

"Is that what you want? Something you can't find in a library?"

"Not precisely. She told us that in exchange for this text, you hired her to craft a hook binding in Granada, Spain. I wish to know who asked you to do that and how you knew to place it there."

Weaver scoffed. "I thought you had a job for me. You're asking me to reveal client information. I don't do that."

"I'll pay handsomely. Was it the Goblin Lords?"

"Just said I don't do that. Word gets out that client information is for sale and I won't have any more clients. If you ever have real business to conduct, we can talk some more. Otherwise we're done here. I got nachos."

"We are not finished, Mr. Weaver. I can't leave here without that information."

"Then I guess you won't be leavin' here. Try anything and my boys will give you an asswhuppin' you won't ever forget."

"I have no fear of your spriggans. They're here illegally, by the way. I'll be informing the sigil agents."

The Weaver's eyes widened a bit at that. "That wasn't very smart. Guess you ain't fought one in a while. Open season, boys." I brought my hands out of my pockets in guard position, knuckles ready, and gave myself the same strength and speed bindings I gave to Slomo.

Slomo, if ye get a chance, I need ye to leap down on top of one of these cowboys and ram your claws into his skull as hard as ye can. Remember he's not human.

<Okay, Oaken!> she replied as cheerfully as if I'd asked her to enjoy her favorite thing. I dropped her camouflage so that I'd be able to see her if she joined in.

"Make sure they're in no condition to talk afterward," Weaver added, before turning on his boot heel to head back indoors.

Coriander was on my left and he moved even further left and toward the door in a strategic move that worked out perfectly for about two whole seconds. The first spriggan pivoted and launched a punch at him, but the herald's kinetic wards took all that force and multiplied it in the opposite direction, sending the muscle backward into the other one who was squaring up against me, wondering what damage my knuckles would do. They tumbled to the ground together, leaving both doors open, and I shifted to block the nearest one. I wanted them in the patio area where Slomo might be able to reach them. Coriander floated on inside after Weaver, leaving me to face two pissed-off spriggans rolling to their feet. They're tough to kill in most cases, so I didn't feel like I had to pull my punches. I let fly at the nearest one right in the sternum, choosing a target they wouldn't easily be able to dodge, but they almost avoided the blow anyway, juking to my right. My punch glanced off their ribs instead with an audible crunching sound and the spriggan flew backward, fetching up against a picnic table along the fence. That gave the other one pause; they had clearly never seen a human do that before. They took a step back, a bit more cautious, and that's when Slomo pounced.

Sloths are not ambush predators and have no grace to speak of. They're mostly forearms and claws with tiny back legs meant to hang on instead of jump. All the juice I was giving her allowed her to perform extraordinary feats for a sloth, but due to her lack of experience or evolutionary suitability, she nearly missed. She technically did miss, I guess, her body falling beyond the spriggan's back, except that the claws of her right hand dug into the meat where the neck meets the collarbone, ground on the actual woody surface there underneath the glamour, and that gave her purchase. She used it to whip her body around counter-clockwise until her form rose like a furry sun over the spriggan's left shoulder, her left forearm and wicked claws leveled at the side of their head. Those claws were designed to get the better of trees. She shoved them with a mighty crack right into the side of the spriggan's head and they went down with her riding them all the way to the ground.

Ah, that's me fine murder sloth! Good job, love.

<Wheee! Thanks, Oaken!>

The other spriggan was getting to their feet, the cowboy glamour melting a little bit, but the expression was clearly shocked at their friend's abrupt death and also in some pain. I'd shattered a wooden rib or two for sure. I didn't want them coming after Slomo, so I stepped forward to meet them.

A random voice from the direction of the taco truck said, "What the shit?" but I didn't have time to worry about whoever that was. I imagined they'd seen some bar fights in their time but probably never one involving a fast-moving sloth with a one-punch deathblow.

This time the spriggan wasn't going to wait for me to strike. They were cornered and desperate and behaved like it. They charged and connected, a fist cracking a rib and stealing my breath, and then a left hook that would have taken off my head if I hadn't ducked. As it was, that glamoured fist concealed fingers ridged with sharp spurs and splinters, and these raked across the top of my scalp and gashed deeply enough that I felt the blood leaking out instantly. I pistoned my fist into its ribs, punching right through them this time and into some warm, sappy organs. The spriggan convulsed and pounded once on my back but then shuddered and died. I lowered my arm and let it fall off onto the ground, turning my head to see Coriander dragging a hollering and flailing Weaver back into the patio area. That was under control; the taco truck wasn't. Greta and the other werewolves of her pack—Sam and Ty especially—had impressed on me the importance of securing the cell phones of any witnesses to "our rarefied shit."

A sloth assassin would generate enough bad publicity, but watching two cowboys melt into vaguely humanoid piles of driftwood and sap would really draw the worst kind of attention. We couldn't risk pictures or videos getting out into the world. If they had everything set to upload automatically to the cloud it might already be too late, but hopefully that wasn't the case.

<Hey Oaken, where you going?>

Be right back.

I burst into the taco truck where a man wearing a bandana on his head cussed at me but eventually surrendered his phone in response to a broken finger when he tried to cut me with a greasy knife.

"Thanks," I said. "Ye can't have this back, but I don't want to have ye feel the loss too keenly." I pulled out an emergency stash of bills that Greta had me carry around for situations like these. I counted out ten Benjamins, since Greta said such a sum soothed over many hurt feelings, and left them on the prep area littered with shredded lettuce. "That should buy ye a new phone. Sorry about the finger, though."

I pocketed the phone and returned to the patio, ignoring the man's swearing.

<This man turned into sticks and sticky stuff and I don't like it,> Slomo said, dragging herself away from the spriggan's remains. <Is this one of those orgies you were talking about?>

No.

<Can I hop on your back again?>

Not yet, love. We might have some more trouble.

Even though Coriander had firmly planted a foot in the chest of Weaver, pinning him in the dirt, and his thrashing was completely ineffective, he was refusing to cooperate. He was either counting on someone to come to his rescue or he simply wasn't scared enough. I didn't think anyone inside would hear him over the volume of the music—no one had come to investigate so far. In case he wasn't scared enough, I thought a shape shift to a bear might be in order. It would ruin me clothes, but it wouldn't be the first time I'd had to streak through a public area today.

Handing over the confiscated phone and some remaining cash to Slomo to guard, I bound my shape to a black bear. When I shifted, bursting through my clothing and roaring in Weaver's face, replacing Coriander's boot with my paw on his chest, a brass-coated claw tickling the hollow of his throat, he may have ruined his clothes too, judging by the fear in his voice and the sudden stench of urine in my nose.

"We don't want your life," Coriander reminded him. "We don't want much at all. Just the name of who hired you to set up an ambush of Javier and Maria Garces."

"You wouldn't believe me if I told you," Weaver protested.

"I might, though. Give me something to confirm, at least, and we can all go about our business and you can go finish your nachos. Was it the Goblin Lords?"

"It's…ahh…it's someone dead."

"You were hired by someone dead?"

"Yeah. It happens sometimes. More often than I'm comfortable with, really."

"How does it happen?"

"Sometimes spirits remember things from their lives. Important information someone alive is willing to pay for. So if you can reach them and give them something they want, it's a great way to find what once was lost, y'know? I had a living client who really wanted to know some details about the Salem Witch Trials—something not in the histories. And I found a soul in hell who was willing to provide those details in return for this ambush."

Coriander's fists clenched at his sides. "Are you talking about a Puritan woman?"

"Yeah. Creepy lady who called herself Goody Goodneck, of all things. How did you know?"

Coriander purpled and got really close to exploding.

CHAPTER 9

shifted back to human so that I could talk properly, even though it meant someone might misinterpret what was going on.

"Let me get this sorted," I said. "You're doing great, by the way, so don't stop talking. Tell us what we need regarding this and you'll walk away safely. What I'm hearing is this: Someone wanted Salem Witch Trials information and you went to Goody Goodneck in hell to get it, and she said her price for that information was setting up a hook binding in Spain?"

"Almost," Weaver admitted. "She wanted someone close to Coriander to die—who and how it was done was up to me. I didn't know anything about him except his title, so I paid a pixie to follow Coriander around and that's how we chose the Garces and knew when they'd be in Spain. After that I contracted Ecne. Favors for favors, that's my game. I didn't talk to Goody Goodneck myself, or do anything except connect clients and services."

"What happened to the pixie you paid?"

"She accidentally ran into some iron after she reported."

"And how was that accident arranged?"

"An owl familiar of a Cornish witch who owed me brought her in for debriefing. She told the witch about the Garces and where they'd be and then…the end."

That explained why that pixie had left her handkerchief on the branch; she'd tried, fruitlessly, to escape an owl with its own magical powers.

Coriander spat in the Weaver's face. "I cannot do any more harm to you than this, for I am bound by rules of conduct. But you will never receive any favors from me, and I will do my best to reduce your custom. Your business of connecting clients and services hurts innocent people."

I wasn't bound by any rules of conduct except Gaia's. I could give the Weaver a bruise or five, maybe a scar or three, but I didn't want to earn the enmity of a man who was obviously well connected and had so many beings owing him favors. And in truth, it wasn't any of my business or my responsibility. Getting involved in shite like this is what led Siodhachan to get in so much trouble. I had apprentices to teach.

"Thank ye, sir," I said, rising from the ground and standing back. "I think we have what we need and I hope you're not hurt. As promised, you're free to go because I'm playing nice. I hope ye won't seek to escalate things and find out what happens when I play for keeps." I gestured to the dead spriggans behind me just to make sure he got the point. He nodded weakly, said nothing, and wiped the spittle from his face.

"We'll be leaving now. Please remain here until we've exited the building."

I turned my back on him as he sat up and walked over to Slomo, taking the phone and cash back from her.

Up and away, love. We're going to take ye home for a proper dangle in the jungle.

<Oh, great! I can get some proper leaves!>

She climbed up on my back and I grunted at the weight, my cracked ribs complaining.

<You're bleeding, Oaken!>

I know, I said gently. *I'll try to stop.*

I set my body about the business of healing, and then cast camouflage on us both so that Jimmy and the other customers wouldn't see me parading past them in the nude.

Coriander got a few stares as he exited with me, but no one commented and no one in the main bar was any wiser about what happened on the patio. I decided I'd come back to the White Horse with Greta soon for some dancing and maybe a shot of Dragon Spit.

Outside in the parking lot, Coriander stopped, a bleak expression on his face, and I urged him to talk as we walked back to the cemetery. I didn't want to be around to meet any reinforcements the Weaver might be able to summon.

"Go ahead and talk," I said to the herald, keeping pace next to him. "I'm here."

"I…I have no recourse."

"No recourse? Can't you send a sigil agent, whatever they are, after that guy for having spriggans?"

"Yes. Yes, I can do that and more, and I will. But there's nothing I can do to Goody Goodneck. She's already in hell. I can hardly ask to have her moved somewhere worse. There's no justice to be had for Javier and Maria. They were killed by someone long dead out of spite."

"I kind of skipped past all that in me own timeline, but from what I've heard, it sounds like the Puritans sucked."

"Yes. They did, in fact, suck. A lot."

"I'm sorry that we didn't find an answer ye liked—not sure ye would have liked any answer, really—but at least we found the answer. That's all the help I can give."

"I appreciate it, Eoghan Ó Cinneadie. Displeasing and disappointing as it is, I would not have found out anything without your help. You have gone out of your way and suffered some injury to aid me. Is there some service I can provide for you?"

I considered for a few steps and then replied, "There is. Can ye have someone weave an Old Way to Slomo's forest and to my place in Flagstaff? Shifting planes via tethered trees makes her vomit, but she can handle the Old Ways just fine. It would let us hang out together more often."

"I can do that. Ecne is in my debt right now. Consider it done."

"Kind of ye. And hey, Coriander?"

"Yes?"

I extended my hand to him. "Ye may have many enemies out there, but I hope ye know I'm not one of them. In fact, I'd consider you a friend if ye have room for one."

He eyed my hand suspiciously, suspecting a trap. "A friend?"

"Sure." I jogged my arm once up and down, keeping it extended for him. "I know I'm about as nice as one of those badger men, but unlike them I can use me words, and so I'm sayin' to ye now that I've grown to like ye, even though we have about as much in common as a peacock and a pile of shite. I'm the shite in that comparison, in case that wasn't clear."

The Herald Extraordinary snorted and a ghost of a smile appeared on his face. "Making me the peacock. Well, I suppose that's fair." He took my hand and shook it, still looking wary, but when I just grinned at him and let go when he was ready, he brightened somewhat. "Thanks, Owen. I like you too."

"Let me know if ye ever feel like kicking some arse recreationally. Ye have to keep practicing or ye lose the talent for it."

He actually chuckled at that. "I will. Farewell, friend."

We returned to Tír na nÓg via the Old Way in the cemetery and parted there. I shifted us back to Slomo's patch in Peru and after she threw up, I told her that she wouldn't have to do that again.

I made a deal to fix that problem so we can travel in the future without you getting sick to your stomach, I told her.

<Oh, that would be good for sure! Thanks, Oaken!>

That was quite an aboblamohno we had, wasn't it?

<Heck yes! I scored First Dangle in many new places and tried some new leaves and helped track down some bad guys, and I learned that the country music never stops in Texas and I even moved fast like a monkey. Did you see me do that?>

I sure did! You were awesome. Here's your tree. You can move like a monkey one more time and get settled in a good spot super fast. Slomo scrambled up the tree and once she had found a satisfactory place to dangle and eat, I removed the strength and speed bindings.

<Thanks for a wonderful day, Oaken. Can't wait to tell my tree about it! It'll get the sap pumping for sure.>

Thanks for hanging out with me, Slomonomobrodolie.

<When will I see you again?> she asked. I didn't know precisely when I'd be able to get away from my teaching duties again, but I surely wanted to see more of the world with her, for she was kind and filled with wonder and that was the sort

of person I wanted to be, having not had as much practice as I should and having plenty of room to grow in that direction.

Soon, love, I told her. *Very soon.*

THE WATERS

This story was originally printed in the Resist *anthology. It takes place an indeterminate time after the events of* Scourged, *Book 9 of the Iron Druid Chronicles.*

Something about running water relaxes me. When I walk alongside a clear mountain stream in the San Juan Mountains of southwestern Colorado, I can forget for a while that the world has a pillow over its face made of gases and that it's smothering to death. It's because the waters never speak of the problems that cause my lips to press into a thin line of worry and my stomach to churn with acid. Instead they ripple and flow over rocks, chuckling as they go, for they're headed downhill and it's easy, and everything they see is brimful of beauty and health, fulsome and fine. I need to forget my problems like that sometimes lest I turn into an Edvard Munch painting, eternally screaming my horror in front of a burning sky. And while I forget, I also remember that long ago, the whole world used to be like the waters, pure and clean and sure of its purpose.

We are far gone from that time now. We can never go home again, as Thomas Wolfe observed. But we can still find thin slices of the primeval tucked away from roads and air traffic corridors and cell phone towers, and taste for a soft sweet while the peace we seek and never find in cities. And if you're a Druid, you can walk among the animals of the world, bind their minds to yours, and feel what it's like to live in blissful ignorance of politics, to drink up the sun or huddle underneath the moon and think of nothing but where to eat next. You can also, if you wish, bind your mind more deeply to a creature and teach them language over time. I have done that with my Irish wolfhound, Orlaith, and she loves roaming through forests with me, sharing what she smells, and asking me to name what it might be, since she's still learning.

<What are these small creatures that are like mice but which aren't mice?>

"You might be thinking of voles or shrews."

<Yes! I think of them often. They aren't as annoying as squirrels, so maybe, if they knew I wouldn't hurt them, we could be friends.>

I grin at her moral compass. "What's worse, Orlaith? Squirrels or cats?"

<Definitely squirrels. They are the worst because even though I have serious disagreements with cats, there are at least some you can get along with. I get along great with you when you're a cat.>

We do have a grand time when I bind myself to the form of a black jaguar and we run through the forest together.

"But you can't ever get along with a squirrel?"

<No, because it's the squirrels who don't want to get along with anybody. They want to hoard everything for themselves and never share. There's no reasoning with them. So that's why hounds always let them know we won't stand for their shenanigans. It's our duty to let them know they're wrong. In fact—look there!>

A squirrel chatters at Orlaith and scurries up a tree as my hound takes off after it, barking like she has serious bad blood with this strange rodent. Even though my hound can stretch to more than six feet tall when she reaches up with her front paws, as she does here, the squirrel quickly outpaces her vertically and reaches safety in a branch above my hound's head. It perches there, looking down, tail twitching, and scolds Orlaith furiously. I let them go at it until Orlaith feels satisfied.

"Okay, now that you've told that squirrel off and they know they're wrong, do you think they'll change their attitude?"

<Not a chance. Look at it. Still thinks it's the boss.>

"Do squirrels ever change their minds?"

<Not that I've ever heard. But if they want to fight about it we'll fight them and win. We can't let squirrels scurry around unchallenged, thinking they're right and they own the forest. We always need to make sure they run and hide.>

"Okay, I can understand that. There are people like that too. Squirrelly, you know, about other people. Internet trolls."

<Oh yes! I've heard of them. You're never supposed to feed them.>

"That's true. I did make one hide though. You'd be proud. Maybe."

"What did you do?"

"This one troll became so famous for being rude on Twitter to women and people of color that he made it into the news. An article I read included some of his tweets, and they were vile, even threatening. Since nothing was being done, I found out which city he lived in and traveled there to talk with the birds."

<Which ones?>

"All of them. I very patiently showed them his picture and said that they should poop on him whenever they saw him. He doesn't go outside much anymore. He can give people shit, but he can't take it, I guess."

THE STREAM WE'RE following is spring runoff high above Silverton, and it's so winsome that we follow it downhill to enjoy it a while longer. It feeds into the Animas River, and soon enough the language of the waters graduates from chuckling and gurgling to a sibilant roar. But the swirls and skirls of it also become sullied by the legacy of mine tailings in the area and a horrible blunder in 2015 that spilled heavy metals into the river from the old Gold King mine. Arsenic, cadmium, and lead, plus copper and aluminum, turned the river orange. It's somewhat better now, but the damage persists, the fish and wildlife poisoned, tourism way down. The miners who exploited the earth long ago for their short-term gain are now dust that could float dispersed among the incalculable damage they did, and that thought crumples the peaceful smile I'd been wearing quicker than failed origami. Because I am hyperaware that we who live today are doing irreparable harm to the world, wiping out species and ruining entire ecologies.

It makes me unbearably sad, and I sit down on the bank, staring at the polluted gunk floating by—much of it unseen, but I can feel it through my connection with the San Juan elemental—and weep for a timeline full of bad decisions.

Orlaith first sits beside me, then lies down and rests her head on my lap for easy petting. It comforts both of us.

<What's wrong?> she says.

"I'm sorry. I just lost it."

<Lost what? Your Zen? Your mojo? Not your shit, I hope?>

"Maybe a little of all three."

<That sounds perilous.>

"It certainly would be for anyone who came along and wanted to start something with me right now."

<What's causing all this loss?>

I flailed an arm at the river. "Witnessing this disaster and knowing it's only one of too many to count. Feeling Gaia in distress. The bugs are dying off, have you noticed? The Great Barrier Reef is toast. There's a huge floating island of plastic garbage in the ocean. Just so much to clean up and everyone thinking that the job is somebody else's problem, never regretting their choices or changing their behavior. Like my stepfather and his oil company."

<But you're fighting him, right? Shutting him down. Because that's something Druids can do.>

"Yes. But it's overwhelming when I think of it. There's so much to do I wonder how I can do anything meaningful in the end."

<I guess I understand that. But you know what?>

"What?"

<Don't tell anybody, but I have never actually caught a squirrel. I don't think I can, if I'm honest. I didn't even get close to that one uphill. But I chase them anyway. I feel morally obligated.>

That makes me laugh through the tears, and I kiss the top of her head for the gift. But it does shift my thinking.

"You're right, of course. 'Whatever I do will become forever what I have done,' so I can't become the Druid who could have done something but chose not to."

<Was part of that a quote or something? Your voice was kind of different.>

"Yes. That's from a poem by the Polish poet Wisława Szymborska. A simple moral reminder to live an examined life. Can you imagine this river, Orlaith, shining and sparkling again, full of healthy fish? It could happen."

<Yeah! It totally could!>

I give Orlaith a final pet and rise to my feet, newly determined. I can't solve what's happening in the halls of government buildings or in the avaricious hearts of soulless men. Those are not powers that Gaia has granted me. But I can do something about making the Animas River run clear and pure again. I can bind the pollutants together and isolate them, prevent more from entering the river, and in so doing revitalize more than a hundred miles of land that will be home and succor for countless animals.

I can do at least this one thing. It may not matter to most of the world but it will matter here, so I will do it. Cleaning up this river, and whatever else I can manage in the time I have, will be forever what I've done.

FRIENDLY EMILY

This is not a part of the Iron Druid Chronicles at all, but rather a flash fiction Sci-Fi story I wrote for Fireside Magazine. *However, I found the encounter so intriguing that I later wrote a novella featuring Emily set some time after this story, and you can enjoy that now: It's called* A Question of Navigation.

Lots of my friends went swimming in whiskey after the election and I may have taken a quick dip myself. Some of them were still swimming—going for distance, I guess. But deadening the pain like that didn't help me cope very well. I rediscovered hiking, going out to see with my own eyes the kind of happy little trees and mountains that Bob Ross used to paint on public television. His landscapes had always been so remarkably free of fascists, and I found that Rocky Mountain National Park was the same.

It was not, I discovered, free of lost children. Five miles away from any trailhead or shuttle stop, high up in the peaks, a young girl examined a carefully picked dandelion in the puffball stage. The park isn't a meat-grinding abattoir like, say, a Los Angeles freeway during rush hour, or the unavoidable Thanksgiving dinner with my racist in-laws, but neither is it completely safe for kids to wander around in all alone.

Dressed in jeans, a pink button-up shirt hanging loose, and barefoot, I estimated her age to be only eight or so. Her dark hair blew idly in a summer breeze announced by the whispery crackle of aspen leaves, framing a heart-shaped face and golden brown skin that might be Mediterranean or a sign of mixed heritage. She beheld the puffball with a pair of large eyes, deep limpid pools of the sort you might see in anime. She heard my boots crunch around the bend in the trail, looked up, and gave a tiny smirk when she saw me stop in confusion.

Instead of saying hello or asking for help, she tried to reassure me. "Don't worry, Mister, I won't eat you," she said. "I'm not hungry right now."

It took me a few beats to respond. That's not a normal greeting to a stranger.

"Are you lost?"

"No. This is Earth, right?"

A fully-developed sense of sarcasm already. "Where are your parents?"

She laughed. "Ha ha! You're funny."

"No, seriously, where are they?"

"They're waiting. They'll pick me up when I'm ready."

"Oh. So they're close by, I hope?"

The girl shrugged. "Depends on what you mean by *close*. May I ask you a question?"

"Of course."

She grinned at me, teeth unusually pointed, I thought, and tossed the puffball over her shoulder before clapping her hands together. "Excellent. This planet appears to be suffering massive extinctions, especially through the acidification of the oceans. Would you say it's because of cyclical natural forces or because of climate change spurred by the short-sighted behavior of your species?"

"My species...? What?"

"Did I not speak clearly? I merely ask because I haven't the time to conduct long-term studies. Our decision-making process would be helped by knowing the answer."

"You spoke clearly, just…not like a child."

She squinted at me. "That's because I'm an adult. Oh, I see! My voice and appearance prevents you from taking me seriously and that's why you asked about my parents. I chose it to be nonthreatening but perhaps I miscalculated. How old do I appear to be to you, Mister?"

"Eight or nine, I guess. How old are you?"

"Forty of your years in subjective time. But I was born centuries ago. Relativistic travel, you know." She smiled at me with those too-sharp teeth.

I started to back away and her face fell.

"Hey, where are you going, Mister? Help me out, here. I promised I wouldn't eat you, remember?"

"I, uh…thanks for that. Really kind of you. But I should probably get back."

"Oh, you have schedule to keep! I understand that completely. But will you answer my question about species extinction? Is it a cyclical phase or your fault?"

"Scientists say it's our fault."

"Ah! Interesting. My brother met someone who said it's natural and self-correcting even though the data doesn't seem to support such a conclusion."

"Well, some people are stupid."

She laughed again, genuine, high-pitched girlish peals bubbling out of her that would have been delightful to hear were she not so clearly something other than a girl.

"Seems like most of you are if you let things get to this point. You're doomed to a corrective die-off. But there should still be plenty of you left to eat when we come back and then we can set up a breeding program for you and probably solve most of the climate problems with carbon traps. It's a beautiful planet and worth cleaning up. Really the jewel of this arm of the galaxy, you know?"

"Well, I—yeah. So, uh. When are you coming back?"

She snorted and waved a dismissive hand at me. "Oh, don't worry, Mister. You'll be dead by then. Enjoy your life and let us think in the long term. But hey, wait, before you go—what do you call these things?" She gently picked another puffball and held it up.

"Those are dandelions."

She blew on it and scattered the seeds in the air, giggling as she watched them float away. "Dandelions are great! I hope they're still around when we come back."

"May I ask…who are you, really?"

"Me, personally? You can call me Emily. That name is supposed to sound friendly. Is it?"

"Friendly? Yes, I suppose it is."

"Perfect. What's your name, Mister?"

"Dennis. But what I meant to ask was, who are your people?"

"Aw, Dennis. You wouldn't be able to vocalize it; I'm sorry. But I can tell you that we're from a yellow sun like yours, except ours is going to expand soon. Yours has seven billion years left, and you guys are *so* delicious. I'm really glad we found you! We've been searching for a sustainable buffet!"

"Right. Super lucky. Well. Gotta go."

She beamed at me and waved. "No problem. Bye, Dennis!"

I sweated and stumbled downhill to my SUV, cutting my hike short. I dropped my keys twice before I could get the door open, my hands shook so much.

"Fuck hiking," I said, my voice broken.

ACKNOWLEDGEMENTS

It must first be acknowledged that sloths are super rad. Secondly, you must confront the fact that *you* are rad. Just sit there and absorb that, soak it all up and let its truth suffuse your being: *you are rad.* I know this because you like Druids and doggies and magic and care about the planet, or otherwise you wouldn't be reading my stuff.

Thanks for reading my stuff, by the way. You deserve a snack.